The Playhouse

THE BOOKS OF
OLUTAYO K. OSUNSAN

Strange Beauty 2004

The Poet in May 2006

The Life of One 2010

The Alchemy of Butterfly Memories 2011

The Life of Another One 2013

Business Communications 2014

This Happiness 2015

Leo 2019

Internationalizing Growth 2020

The Integrity Clause 2021

THE PLAYHOUSE

Olutayo K. Osunsan

The Playhouse

ISBN: 979-8582324843

Cover Design by Olutayo K. Osunsan and KDP

First Edition, July 2024

Printed in USA

For Anne Born
(July 9, 1924 – July 27, 2011)

Thank you for making time for me, inspiring me to write, and offering invaluable life advice. Your encouragement meant the world to me.

"In My Father's house are many mansions; if it were not so, I would have told you. I go to prepare a place for you. And if I go and prepare a place for you, I will come again and receive you to Myself; that where I am, there you may be also. And where I go you know, and the way you know."

—John 14:2-4 (NKJV)

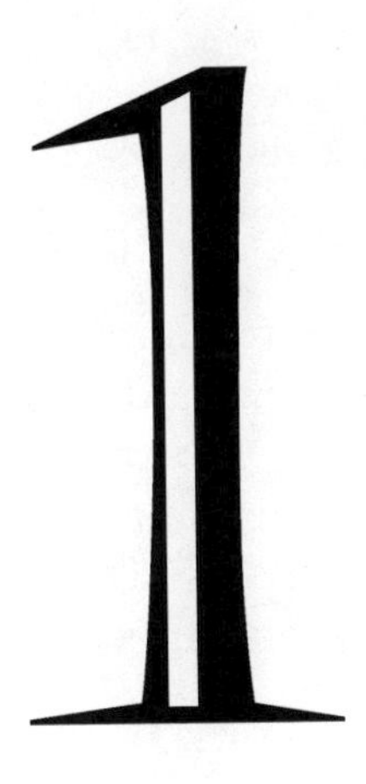

In my father's house, there were very many windows and very few doors. The windows hung tilted, framing breathless views. Every moment of my childhood was captured in each view. He saw a lot but said very little. His memories were frozen in time, like a heavy burden the mind could barely process yet found too sweet to completely forget. The few doors led only to alleyways that promised little, yet my insatiable curiosity always dragged me to open them and see for myself the harsh realities of poverty and the foul breath of its discourse. Walls coloured like the rainbow, they glittered with the splendour of youthful ambitions, teenage wet dreams and regrets of adulthood. The black ceiling mirrored a vast, starlit night, an expanse of unattainable magnificence one could only aspire to, but never truly achieve. My father's house, grand and majestic in the middle of nowhere, held both promise and imperfection, much like myself. I, too, was said to hold promise, but never made sense. All I craved was escape, a way to flee the confines of my life, but to where?

***

What my father spoke of, I do not want to believe. What I thought I knew is what I know and that is the truth to me. My mother stood quietly like a mist in a desert inferno. Though her every gesture conveyed the desire to erase the day, all she could do was eventually yield. The day the thought or conviction to tell me the truth knocked at the door of her heart and turned it amber hot, my father, the more suitable villain spoke slowly, his voice trembling. He summoned his greatest strength from within to maintain composure that would assure my mother everything was under control and not as bad as it seemed. He found no logic or reason in telling me the truth, but my mother could not live with a lie. The truth had to be revealed, a slow descent that eventually reached my ears. It settled deep within me, like silt accumulating on a riverbed. It made everything calm in a halt that precedes a crescendo. I would rather forget it was spoken and that I did, but for sure, something was undeniably broken. I was broken and that is why they told me the truth.

***

They say crazy people have crazy stories and wild imaginations. They can see things that are not there and recall events that never happened. They even know people that no one else knows. Koto, my old gardener, must have been crazy. He used to tell me how his great-grandmother indulged his grandfather, under the cool twilight of African moons when he was a child, that life was a series of houses. She told him, under the shelter of her gaze and the consolation of her voice, that he must always strive to emancipate himself from each house he found himself in. The older one got, the more windows there would be and the more views one would have on life and the better understanding of the past mingles with certain uncertainness of the future. According to her, every now and then, one would proceed to the next house and windows would continue to appear in each new house. One's views on life would broaden with more awareness to the things that go unspoken. Koto recounted in bewilderment as to how two grownups can rise in the rage of the vilest beast and want to end each other's existence, or why a man so intoxicated by the serum of love would be willing to throw his life away to protect a love that never was really his. Koto's great-grandmother used to tell him that there were five houses, according to their culture, every human would have to go through before reaching 'the Grand Fields of the Ancestors'. She acquainted him with the belief that they would go through the stages: as a baby in ‘the womb house'; as a child in ‘the sleep house'; as a teenager in ‘the playhouse'; as an adult in ‘the workhouse' and finally as an elder ‘the wisdom house'.

When one leaves the wisdom house, the afterlife awaits, and then they shall truly be free. Koto described the Grand Fields of the Ancestors as where the dead and wise with grey hair go; they would know everything; the mysteries of the universe would become comprehensible. There, they would not have any mud walls around them as they used to in their former lives, no thatch roofs over their heads, their minds would penetrate through every riddle, and their eyes would see every corner and beyond the horizons. They would know the reason why the sun chases the moon around the sky, why the winds hide their colours, why the ground pretends to be still and why the gods hide their existence among the simple things.

I always asked Koto when I was much younger why I didn't see any mud walls and thatched roofs around me. He always responded by telling me that the mud walls and thatched roofs were symbols that depicted human inabilities, limitations and mindsets that make us prisoners. He claimed that most of the time we didn't know they were there, but they were like our shadows following us through enigmatic hours like a marriage convoy to our grave. He always sounded as though he was talking about someone or something that could fry him with a bolt of lightning and so, he always chose his words with utmost reflection and plucked each with a sanctified hand. The ancestors could be irritated by the choice of words that do not suit the pallet of their delicate ears.

Every time I told him I was confused by his stories and tales, Koto always said I would know more about the mud walls that the house is built with when I left ‘the playhouse'. Smiling at me like the worst was yet to come; his old eyes looked even staler, and when I shrugged in ignorance, he would say ‘though the breath of an elder may be foul, it carries the aroma of wisdom'. I sometimes concluded he had some bolts missing or a short circuit somewhere. My parents concurred.

He always left me clueless and sometimes frightened when he started to talk about his oracular village where animals take human form at night and ghosts return to their homes after their burial; his great grandfather's family's dark past and the superstitions that dictated his every whim. The comical thing was that I always asked him to tell me more. He seemed to know everything and had such a calm reverence and a fervent enthusiasm for the tales that a candlelight temporarily glowed in his dull eyes and made me long to go into his mind and see through his ancient eyes the tales he told so vividly. But could it all be a lie woven to keep my bored eyes off the TV and allow my mind to take a journey with him into a twisted imagination?

***

The inert sun seemed to set with the thick laced clouds subduing its light and the wind seemed to get colder. The noonday breeze was heavier as the clouds gathered a dark shade and grew in texture, sending leaves whirling in the September winds. Across the bushes, beyond the huddling banana trees, where the garden used to be was the old playhouse where my sister and I spent most of our early days. It stood like a lost and lonely church in the middle of an overgrown field, condemned by wicked rains, stripped of its colours by glorious sun shines. My father and Koto built it to look like an 'enhanced' kennel. Father was afraid that we would fall from the tree if he made it a tree house since my sister and I always had arguments that turned physical. In most cases, her dolls suffered the loss of body parts as retaliation for my damaged toys. Shola called it a heap of wood, but I called it the playhouse after Koto's recommendation. It always turned into a fight every time she insisted it was a pile of wood. For me it was the closest I got to the village life experience and a real hut, though there were no mud walls or thatched roofs.

Shola would spend the whole day drinking empty cups of tea with her dolls and mumbling hollow words to them about the smell and the dirt in the hut, while they just remained with their fixed smiles. I always felt sorry for the dolls, the way Shola's shrilling voice would persistently pierce their plastic ears and they were unable to cover their ears or tell her to shut up for a few minutes while they gathered their thoughts on how to gag her and staple her mouth. There were times I would spend the whole day dreaming up how to get Shola out of the playhouse, she would whine about it but spend more time in it than I did. It's no surprise she grew up to become a cynical and critical woman who always undermines everything she holds dear.

I spent most of my time, when not trying to chase Shola out of the playhouse, building and breaking down wooden blocks; back then I knew I wanted to be the greatest architect, even better than my father. I knew it would make him the proudest man on earth and he made the most of every opportunity to take me to work with him to see blueprints and computer-animated projections of apartment blocks, malls and office buildings. We always spent the first few hours going from cubical to cubical with everyone remarking 'is this Tola, your son?', 'he has really grown up',' What do you feed him?' My father would beam as though he had made a huge return on an investment while patting me on the back. I always pondered if father noticed that most of the people, we met were not really bothered about how I had grown or anything like that, they just wanted to make him feel good and be seen in the radiance of his favour since he was the boss.

Those days were the greatest times in my life, everything felt like a feel-good movie; there was nothing to worry about. It made my breathing pause and I started to wonder exactly when Koto died; it haunts me, Koto in a lonely place dying alone. I always pictured him alone in the middle of an angry sea, gasping for air, reaching out to someone or anyone. I always wondered what was on his mind; who he was thinking of or what he was thinking of and maybe everything started to fade out like a drowning sensation in a dream. His laboured spirit leaving his body swinging away into the next life or wherever. Did he look back? Was he in pain? And is he in heaven or in the Grand Fields roaming free like an animal in the Garden of Eden without a single worry, regret or grudge? Where could he be now? I miss him sometimes when I'm home alone in summer holidays and the TV seems to be in a loop. I miss his stories, his respectful voice to the things he thinks he knows he knows. I am unsure of everything, except my name. Koto always had the answers. I wish he were here. He would probably say some senseless things that would make sense in a senseless way and make everything better.

My eyes caught the birds' nest that was on the mango tree, located next to the huddling banana plants. The nest used to be crowded with eggs, but now the eggs had hatched and the chicks had flown away. All that was left was their mother and occasionally, their father, I think. The two birds spend their time together twittering away, as their once yellowish-grey feathers seem to fade into a lighter shade. I felt guilty that I used to stone the nest. I recall once when I was twelve; one of the eggs popped out the nest and broke on the shrub. The partly formed bird in the cracked egg seemed like it was having seizures, its huge black eyes stared at me like it was calling for help. I remember poking it with a stick and light red blood viscously poured out as its tiny wings quivered one last time before it died. I felt so fulfilled that day like I had discovered a new mystery about the universe, the power to poke and take a life. I wish I hadn't done that and craved undoing it. Koto told me the day I killed the bird that the ancestors would punish me for the heartless act; the bird was sacred to his tribe and he claimed some of his ancestors were birds. I laughed at him and Shola laughed as well, though she said I was heartless for killing the poor little *birdie.* I truly was. Shola claimed those were the first signs showing I would one day become notoriously famous as a serial killer and make Jack the Ripper envious.

My thoughts drifted back to the playhouse. It was old and the strange coloured wood was like fish scales, cracked with droughts of years and winds slapping against its former primary colour shades. Except for some wooden blocks and some of Shola's half buried old dolls, it was quite empty. The dolls must be having the time of their lives, enjoying the silence, the wind sweeping leaves, birds and insects playing hide and seek under the beautiful days of the sun dancing with the hours.

Shola lives in her own house now, far away from her dolls and the playhouse. She spends her days cuddling her infant and gossiping on the telephone with her cronies about former classmates, ex-boyfriends and the ‘dogs’ men really are. She seems like she never played with dolls or hung around in the little wooden house built by father for both her and I. It seemed unthinkable that she ever ran around the backyard almost naked when I was chasing her with the dead bird, threatening to smear her with the blood. I don't think she remembers who Koto was or what the playhouse smelled like after it had rained. The way light rays cut through the panes of the playhouse like lightsabres. When she came by a few weeks ago, she did not even get out of the car because father was home and she told mother and I to come visit her and gave us her new address. Shola is too busy hating men, going through them like a bottle of vodka and making them want to leave her to rot. She once hit a boyfriend on the head with a bottle when she found him having sex in the bathroom at a club, they went to together to celebrate New Year's Eve. She spent New Year's Day in jail and brewed her resentment towards men by the way she was assaulted there by the prostitutes she shared the cell with. To Shola, all the problems in the world are caused by men and men alone, but still, it seems she can't resist a typical bad boy. She once told me that men who are daring, exciting and are not restrained by rules make her always say ‘yes' to whatever they want.

I wondered if she or I would come back to find the playhouse still there waiting for us like it always did when we went to school. I wondered if the birds come back to see their parents; I wondered if the birds in the backyard would ever have their offspring come to visit. I wondered if they were the same birds whose unhatched chick I killed or some other ones that found an empty nest. If they were the real parents, I wondered if they still remembered that I was the one who killed one of their chicks. Their little *birdie* would have grown up to be a great bird, the darling of the bird world, the heartthrob of every girl and the hopes of all their promises. They probably wish God pokes me to death too the way I did their little *birdie.*

I never thought a time would come when I would have to leave the playhouse. It was all I ever had that was truly mine; it was my refuge in many troubles. Hiding from mom’s wrath or avoiding unwanted visitors. When I was too big and much older to fit in the playhouse, I always sat in the backyard and replayed all the memories hoping it would spill over into whatever it was that was dragging me into sadness. It reminded me of Koto; it consoled me when Christie dumped me; it helped me deal with the news of my parent’s illness.

As Koto told me the last time we met, about three years back, if I don't go to the world outside, the world outside will come to me. I would have to learn what I have always avoided, the truth about life and its complexity; he came up with those revelations when I asked him about how to graft a plant. I never thought death would visit us so soon and in such a way, now it hovers and lives with me, its life draining fists knock at doors and its presence, smell and voice can be heard in our home. The hospital visits, the weight loss, the stares and the constant nodding of doctors and nurses when they pass by us in the hallway as we wait for our mother. Father would be silent on the way back home and focus on the driving as though he was doing a driving test. Mother would try to chat, hiding her weariness under shallow laughs and questions with obvious answers. Shola and I would seat at the back of the car, my heart pounding and

Shola looking plain like a whiteboard. Sometimes I fear it was the bird I killed that brought all this, maybe it was Koto's ancestors trying to punish me for the poor bird. Maybe it's God answering the cry of *birdie's* parents. Maybe it's God poking at my life with a stick.

"Tola, your taxi is here; Boko will be waiting for you at the airport …hurry up, time to go…" my mother called from the echoes of my room where she had been packing the whole week. She said it was her last opportunity to get the feeling I'm still a kid like I'm going on one of my school field trips to return in a week. She packed snacks and gave me some of her 'side money' in case I needed something that my upkeep could not cover. I could hear the despair in her doleful voice, I wasn't sure if it was because I was leaving or because I had spent the last two hours staring at the playhouse instead of telling her how much I'll miss her, but whatever it was, my mother is a strong woman.

She will probably keep the tears till I am gone. I guessed she was afraid the other students would have a negative influence on me, I would not be safe anywhere far away from her or something might go wrong somewhere, like all mothers do that is why she made sure Boko and I were on the same flight, to ensure that I had someone responsible with 'God' in his life around me.

Heading back to the backyard entrance, I took one more glance at the playhouse and the whole backyard, it was beautiful and it still reminded me of Koto. I could not believe my eyes betrayed me, they were damp and it seemed as if I was leaving a part of myself behind as if I was breaking away from an addiction that gave me all the strength and courage I needed. I felt I was becoming vulnerable. If my mother had seen me crying, she definitely would have cried too. I had to stop. It felt as though I was doing what was wrong, but would not admit it because I am not sure if I was.

The air was crowded with rain droplets and the banana trees stood trembling in their misty sites, leaving the mango tree in solemn darkness, with its branches waving gently at the air. The now greyish bushes bent their heads to the passing breeze as dead leaves rode the heavier breeze to their uncertain destinations. In the distant sky, the sluggish sun crept behind moist early evening clouds slowly to its next location as birds darted after its fading light.

"Tola, the taxi is waiting…you are going to be late"

All her attempts to make me reconsider had failed. I told her

I was going to Uganda to study and for no other reason. My father told her to let me be, that I needed space. Sadly, all the space in the world would not do. Something was broken!

The only thing that kept me ashore from the gloomy depths of depression and the possibility of suffocation was the stinging stench of tobacco and unwashed body odor emanating from the taxi driver. I was seated in the back, but his endless chant about the growing traffic, crime rate in Nairobi and the good days in Africa, was history at its worst.

Words failed me. I yearned for the solitude of the car's rocking rhythm, but that was a luxury I could not afford.

Rain lashed against the windows, and while I wouldn't have minded getting wet, I worried about the driver complaining about his seats.

He possessed a fervor akin to Koto's for what he called 'true African values'. Koto believed that the moral fabric of Africa had totally deteriorated under foreign influence. Everybody wanted to be like people on TV, and no one had respect for their elders. The girls were half-naked and the boys were chasing each other for love, he lamented.

When Christie and I had been together, Koto claimed I was going out with her because I hated my own colour, my own kind. That every black person in the world hated themselves because they'd been programmed to believe black was bad and white was good.

He said every white person knew in their hearts that blacks were inferior and would always remain so, but they just didn't say it. All Africa's problems were caused by the Europeans, Asians, Americans, but not Africans themselves, he constantly maintained.

Every time Christie and I went out, I always wondered what she was thinking and why she was going out with me. I always nagged her for an answer. I asked her what she thought about the slave trade, colonization of Africa, the United Nation's delay to interfere in the Rwanda genocide, and the negotiating power of third world countries in international trade matters.

She said I was boring her. I wasn't sure if I was really boring or she was just trying to avoid the question, but I hurt her feelings several times with my irritating connotation and insinuations.

On my fifteenth birthday, my grand romantic gesture of proposing was met with rejection veiled as 'we are too young'. I interpreted it as a 'no' and told her she didn't want to marry me because I was black. That did it.

Christie was offended and said she was insulted by my racist attitude. She did not speak to me for a week.

I had Pete, the class bully to help me tell her I was sorry, but instead, he stole her from me. Pete brought me a 'Dear John' letter from Christie and I cried the whole day in the school cafeteria.

I remember a first or second grader asking why I was crying. Her tiny voice had tried to console me by offering me a cheesecake from her lunch box but I totally ignored her and didn't bother looking at her. She wore *Hello Kitty* shoes.

Later, I overheard her telling her friends on the other table I was probably new in school because 'big boys don't cry in the school cafeteria'. Her friends agreed and one even thought I was probably missing my 'mummy' because the same happened to her on her first day of school.

Thinking of it now, I feel so stupid, but then, it seemed the world had just ended. I found Pete and Christie hanging out at the Carnivore, and cried some more there and then; that night, I took up drinking.

I tried begging her, but she told me Pete told her about how I believed white people hated all blacks and I was racist. I confronted Pete, trying to fight to get my girl back, but he beat me up every time, first at the Valentine's dinner dance, the football field, the changing room and finally at the assembly where Shola came to my rescue.

The whole school nicknamed me 'Pete's feet,' because he stomped on me after tackling me to the ground like a seasoned rugby player.

The name stuck 'til I left high school, I was known as an extension of Pete's feet, all in the name of Christie.

I loved Christie, her alto voice, the way she smiled at me like a sunflower, the yellowish-brown colour of her hair, the freckles on her Nordic face and the way she smelled like a beauty soap mixed in a pool of woody moss fragrances.

I loved her.

"Africa is being troubled by those white people, they come here and steal our good things; they steal the brains after they drain them, even the election violence," the driver ranted in Swahili, slamming his fist on the steering wheel. "Now all the young boys don't want to stay at home anymore. They all want to go there."

His disrespect for my thoughts of Christie made me question his conspiracy theories. After accusing some of the tribes in the country for having all the good jobs, he droned on about the premier league and how it made his weekends along with a cold bottle of beer or local brew depending on what his wallet dictated. He accused Manchester United of bribing referees and swore that up to twenty-seven Kenyans played in the premier league, but by different names and nationalities.

"Can you realize, in 1942 when the African continent was still under the…" the man paused for a gasp of air.

I sighed, feeling like Shola's abandoned dolls at that moment.

The peace of raindrops knocking on the car's body like fans wanting a glimpse of their favourite star driving into a movie premiere was comforting. It felt like the rain, forever separated from the cozy world within the car, longed for a glimpse of the passengers, a fleeting interaction to break the monotony.

The star peaceful in his cozy car, staring at copycats and cheap clothes with hands waving, willing to buy anything his name was on.

"Sir, I didn't want to interrupt your interesting opinion on Africa, but I'm in a hurry," I tried to explain with a little flattery and respect to his delight in broken Swahili.

He was flattered; I saw the formation of a smile on his face from the reflection in the rearview mirror. “How did you know I was a lecturer?” he asked in tattered English, obviously noticing I was a foreigner, at the same time changing the topic about my time.

“Before 1954, after finishing my colonial service under Right-Captain…” he paused “at Fort Jesus in Mombasa, I lectured for ten years in the university. I was the only black lecturer at that time, as a matter of sincerity. I was the one who encouraged more African lecturers in that place.” He gestured out the window, creating the illusion that the university was just a stone’s throw away.

He claimed he worked as a prison guard in Fort Jesus in Mombasa and used to live around Mtwapa in Kilifi county, around the area where the new prison was built. The taxi driver explained the new prison was called *Shino La Tewa* prison and it replaced Fort Jesus as a prison in 1958.

Like I cared.

He gave dates and times and events that kept rolling through my ears and out the other end.

I think he felt he had obligation to entertain me with conversation as part of the service he was providing.

“When Her Majesty the Queen of England was here, I was invited as a guest speaker to explain ‘The correlating pinnacles on the moral fabric of the British Empire in contrast to the supreme diplomacy of the ancient African kings’. It was a research paper I wrote when I was a first-year honours student at the Cambridge University in Scotland. The Queen was to give me a Knighthood for that body of work.”

I had to try to pretend I had no idea where Cambridge University was located, and drew the conclusion everything he said was probably nothing but lies. “Sir, I said I am going to the airport, Jomo Kenyatta International Airport. You just missed the turning!" I tried to remain composed though my tolerance was running dry.

“Yes, I remember! I am old but my head is still good. There is a new shortcut there…to Embakasi." He pointed again to where he was turning as though he could not see since the rain was fogging the window’s shield.

"Turn on the AC to clear the fog out," I commanded also running out of regard for him.

"Which fog is that?" he looked back pretending not to notice the car windows are foggy. I pointed to the windscreen in front of him and he passed me a soiled rag to wipe my window while he used his palms to clear the windshield.

"The AC will eat my fuel and it is almost finished," he said as if he was grumbling and continued with his bogus tales. "Can you believe I was the youngest Member of Parliament in 1981, I am sure you were not born then…" he giggled proudly. His lies seemed to flow with the rhythmic swing of his car wipers which screeched at every motion. On the dashboard, he had a partly torn brown stick saying 'Hakuna Matata', but the 'ta' was missing.

I felt goosebumps all over when I saw the Airport signboard; I realized I was getting closer to Uganda and farther away from home. When we got to the departure block in the airport, the taxi finally stopped. The driver turned round in his seat and stared at me as if he was suspicious. He smelled like damp tobacco, his leather jacket seemed to have been made of tobacco leaves. Rubbing his dark beard with a rugged grace as though he had been through life ten times over and had seen it all, he gave a shallow smile. The darkened colour of his head and beard showed evidence of cheap hair dye. The parting in his hair reminded me of the old black and white photos of Nelson Mandela that appear in the media every now and then.

"What is the matter?" I asked thinking he wanted more money than we agreed. I realized what he was up to as he revealed the mosaic of his tobacco-studded teeth that made me doubt if he would ever have the privilege of kissing a lady again.

"Now you are in the airport and about to head for the good pastures, I would like to advise you; you know in Africa: 'the whole village is the father of a child,'" He tried to justify with a proverb. "I know you are not from these parts, but you have good manners. When you get to America, don't become American, remember who you are and remember your family. If you are carrying drugs, you better leave them here in my car. You study hard. Make good money. Don't impregnate anybody and make sure you send your parents money". He paused for what seemed like an hour staring into my eyes and thus creating the most awkward of silences. The taxi driver's eyes looked like they were held in their sockets by the strings of red veins that splattered across them, hoisting them like Spiderman's web. To limit the awkwardness, I thanked him for his advice and told him that I will keep it close to my heart. He in return told me that a word of advice could not be cherished without the exchange of money to value it, I gave him an additional five shillings and he looked puzzled.

Though there was the option of changing in the Forex Bureau, I thought of spending my last few shillings on a phone call to Shola or maybe Christie. Christie had been in town for holidays and would be going back in two weeks. I had last saw her in Eldoret, cycling with her sister. I wanted to pass by to greet her but I was afraid she might have forgotten me, or she'd remember I was her racist ex-boyfriend in high school. I really wanted to see her face and her smile again but I knew I was going to mix up the words and end up making her thank God she was no longer my girlfriend. I tried resisting the urge to call Christie, but my effort was futile.

The phone's light was too bright irritating the eyes, I put on my shades from the backpack and placed my feet on my suitcase. The phone rang and someone picked it up, sounded like her father.

"Good evening, sir. May I please speak to Christie?"

"Sure. Hold on," I heard him call her name."

"She's coming"

"Thank you"

On the phone, I heard the sound of her feet thumping down the stairs drowning out the TV. My heart hammered around my ribs as though it wanted out. A guy that looked like Boko stood outside the building in the distance and went back in after a few minutes. The taxi driver hooted, I waved and he drove off in his Toyota Corolla, leaving a lot of exhaust fume behind.

There was a swift grab on the other end of the phone.

"Hello?"

"Hi!" I almost choked on my spit. My tongue felt like lead and my whole mouth stopped functioning.

"Hi. Who is this?" Christie demanded in her tranquil voice, but I did not know what to respond. "Your boyfriend in the 10th grade, Me, Tola, I saw you in Eldoret the other day or I am thinking of you". I didn't know which, so I kept silent and tried to remember her pretty smell. The same scent she wrapped my birthday gift in.

"Hellooooooo?" she called out teasingly, which made me smile, "Ok, I'm hanging up." but I hung up before she did. It made me feel we had a healthy conversation and I felt we already caught up from where we left off. I said sorry, she said its ok and I said I still love her and she said she still loved me too, though I only said hi.

I wanted to call Shola, but I was afraid I would miss my flight and there was a high chance she wasn't home. I dialed Christie's number again, but the line was busy. As I walked towards the entrance of the building, the thought strolled into my head that she was probably calling her new boyfriend. Someone more mature and possibly refined. Definitely not Pete. She couldn't go out with a ‘blockhead' like that for too long. She probably went out with him to spite me for being such an ass, which I probably still am. The only difference is that I am now a truly messed up ass who doesn't know where he really belongs.

Boko waved, trying to get my attention. His haircut, high in the front with a wide parting on the left side, always stood out, a remnant of his father's younger days perhaps. Boko was one of those guys I had limited interaction with. A few words within class initially. I asked him for a pen in the 8th grade while doing a history quiz, he asked me what the matter was in the cafeteria when Christie broke up with me in the 10th grade, and his parents gave me a lift to our graduation because my mom was admitted to the hospital and my father was nowhere to be found. I asked my father why he was such a womanizer and why he was not falling sick like my mother was. The stare in his eyes felt like a punch in my face and I could see jaw bones pulsating with compressed anger. He turned around without a word and walked away with disappointment arched over his shoulders. He left me in the hospital with my mother. I thought I would stay with her in the hospital, but she insisted I go for the graduation. All my effort to call Shola failed. Her phone was ringing, but she never answered. My father's phone was off. Throughout the drive, Boko's parents, aware of my situation, tried to make a conversation.

"How does it feel, finally leaving high school?" Boko's mother inquired with the voice of a French film star.

"Fine".

"You must be looking forward to university. Freedom from home. Yes?" His father chipped in.

"Yes".

For the duration of the trip, Boko sat there next to me lost in thought. I caught his mother trying to make eye contact with him, probably to prompt him to say something nice or funny to me.

Mother always said she would meet him in church, and he always sent his regards. When she found out he was also going to study in Uganda, she decided to make me leave with him. For the past two months, we have hanged out, not really as friends but as people with a common future. The same way tourists will stick together in a foreign land as long as they speak the same language, though they never met before and will most likely never meet again after the trip.

The boarding announcement for our flight had just been made as I stumbled through the departure lounge and Boko seemed ecstatic in anticipation of the journey. The voice of the announcer seemed like she held her nose when she spoke and she did so in a hurry. I tugged my path through the idle crowd in the lobby: a group of people dressed like Masais, though only two of them appeared to be real Masais; some backpackers in grubby outfits smoking Marlboro, clergies just standing by and families in clusters laughing about God knows what. Boko's seat was immediately taken as he rose to pick his bags; he smiled at the stout lady in a denim jacket and she smiled back in embarrassment at pouncing on his seat. She opened a Nation newspaper and started reading to cover her face.

I pulled out my passport and ticket from the smallest compartment of my backpack and the disc man almost fell out. Some of the tourists standing by looked at it as if it was a radio cassette Walkman. Boko came still smiling in his usual Fanta commercial demeanour. He shook my hand as if we were just meeting for the very first time, his height made him appear like he was stooping. My suitcase was checked in by the lady in the Kenya Airways uniform behind the counter. She had a pleasant smile that distinctly told me I needed to move fast. Asking if I had everything, Boko and I quickly proceeded to boarding. A baffled expression overtook Boko's smiling face as we walked through the departure terminal. I assumed he must have picked up the smell of tobacco on my clothes, but I wasn't bothered about what he thought. I was bothered about the taxi driver, how he got that deep into tobacco and what he was really like. His life, if he had a son, a wife or maybe a daughter. What would happen to them if anything happened to him, like an attack by armed robbers or a car accident and his empty body spread out in his own blood? How long would it be before they discovered he was missing? Would they think he is gone like he usually does for weeks and comes back to tell them stories of his passengers, the Nigerian boy, the prostitutes who didn't pay, the white tourist couple who gave him a hundred dollars, the pregnant woman who nearly gave birth in his car and her daughter who just kept saying 'sorry mommy' and many others that he had transported to bars, clubs, hotels, airport, and even hospitals? I was bothered that he had the kindness to hoot and wave me 'goodbye', sending his good wishes along with me on my journey. People are not made to be kind. They are just made.

"Lovely", Boko remarked as he finally leaned back comfortably in his seat, ready for the short flight. His composure was that of a first-class passenger: a composed arrogance with an air of loftiness. The mode of his voice sounded like the preamble to a conversation, which I might not be interested in. His jeans matched his cap and made him look much older like he was on a business trip to close one of the biggest deals of his career as a budding star. His shoes were glossy like noonday tar reflecting light and traces of starch were evident on his sharp white shirt.

I pretended not to have heard what he said and rudely sat down as though I was upset with the interrogations of the customs officers when I went through security. I used to be upset, but I realized it was just part of the things a Nigerian had to go through when travelling. Departure is the easy part, arrival is worst, the questions are now printed in my memory and I can answer them while thinking of what to have on the plane, 'where are you from?', 'what nationality are you?', 'what Passport do you hold?', 'do you have anything to declare?', 'are you carrying any contrabands?', 'what is the purpose of your visit?', 'what is in your bags?', 'can you open them please?', 'what is this and what is that?', and they continue until I lose my temper and pour out the contents of my bag on the floor. A family friend once told us that she always had her dirty underwears in her suitcase as the top layer. The immigration officers always blushed when they saw the underwears and asked her to proceed immediately. I didn't have the courage to do that, sometimes the officers are pretty and I would like to make the right impression. I remember once in Addis Ababa; the immigration officer was so pretty I gave in to every request without getting upset or irritated. I even recommended a body search to which she laughed and told me I was funny, and said the scanner would suffice. My parents always wondered why I loved going on transit when I can get a more direct flight, but I always gave the excuse that it gives me the opportunity to experience different cultures and to collect stamps from all those countries to add to my stamp collection. They felt it must be very tiring but always made sure I got as much transit time as possible every time they arranged my flights.

"Tola, would you like to pray before the plane takes off?", Boko almost whispered.

"Do you think the plane will crash?" I demanded; an Indian passenger in front snatched a quick glimpse at us, probably unnerved by the word 'crash' on a plane.

"No!"

"I already prayed." I lied. The girl in the opposite row seemed like she was checking me out. She looked South African and praying might freak her out. Her hand with its polished complexion pushed her dark hair behind her ears with the noise of bangles clapping. She had a silver nose ring that made her look sort of Indian. When the guy seating next to her on the side of the window held her hand, I knew she was taken. Christie came to my mind, her hair and the same way she pushed it behind her ears with her index finger.

Boko was praying, while the air hostess displayed the safety procedures in case of an emergency. When Boko finished praying, he still did not pay attention to the briefing, he just kept fidgeting with the seat and the headset. I was irritated. If the plane was crashing, I'd probably not show him how to put on the parachutes and leave him to go down with the plane. I'm not sure if I would be able to remember the procedures, I'd be too frightened to think. I'd just run to the pilot and threaten to choke him to death if he didn't get the engine started. I don't think the air hostesses would still be smiling gingerly and they'd be cursing to passengers and pushing them out of the plane some with parachutes others without. This, of course, was my distorted imagination at work.

"Were you upset about the customs officers?" Boko asked me ignoring the air hostess.

"I can't be. I am Nigerian; they always do that to us." I

informed him.

"Really, but they did the same to me and I'm not Nigerian."

"They did not! He just looked in your bags, but he poured mine out." I tried to remind him.

"No. He actually poured out mine not yours. I think you are just paranoid."

"I never knew you were a psychologist."

"I am not."

"Then mind your own business, Doctor Phil, I'm trying to listen!"

"That's hostile" Boko giggled. I did not respond but I felt like I needed to get him back for pushing my buttons.

We were airborne for a while and the songs on the headphone kept reminding me of Christie and home. One of the Five Alive songs reminded me of when we went climbing Mount Kenya with the class and we stood on Point Lenana. I had it playing on my mp3 and I had Christie's hand in mine; in the distance, Batian and Nelion stood like titans guarding our love. It felt like I was on top of the world that day, Christie with me and the sunrise breaking up into the air through the clouds like a beacon telling us our destiny is together forever. I felt like walking on the clouds that stretched like a vast plain to anywhere I wanted to go. No walls, gates, no need for visas, no one would ask where I am from, I would be free, emancipated from everything that made me lack, everything that turned my inside upside down. Christie was there with me, the picture of us on the mountain peak is always in my wallet. It's like a good luck charm.

Boko successfully managed to call on God and Jesus more times in the plane than I had in my whole life and that made me uneasy; he was sounding like a religious freak. When the plane ran into turbulence, it felt like a free fall and the thought of crashing peeped. Boko, like the other passengers, seemed unmoved and I assumed it was just me being a bad flyer. I nodded as he gave his predictions of our future study experiences, though I had no clue what he was really saying. I was irritated by something, but this time I did not know what. Maybe it was the immigration officers. Maybe it was the boyfriend of the South African who kept squeezing her hands as though she was about to disappear or the thought of not knowing what Kintu is like anymore. Since Boko was very loquacious and I clearly remembered he wanted to go to the States for university, I asked him what had happened, to get him to shut up.

"I was denied the student visa" he replied.

"Because you were a religious fanatic?" I tried to aggravate.

"No, because it's not where God wants me to be."

"What else would you say? 'God wanted me…to be denied'" I mocked in a deep biblical tone.

A large percentage of people who wanted to go to America must have heard, "Sorry, you are not the type of person we want in the United States of America, when you have a more solid reason to travel, please try again. Thank you!" at least once, and at that point, many would realize a few hundred dollars were burnt in fifty seconds, the same amount that could have fed the family back in the village for four months if not more. With the terrorism and terrorist plots, it's close to impossible to get a US visa. I heard of people who changed their names and passports several times, but were still denied.

After queuing in line for hours in the cold and most of the people in the city know, you are trying to go to the US, filling out the complicated forms that make the SATs look like a kindergarten color book, going through humiliating security inspections which might include revealing to the queue that you have condoms ready for anything, and then waiting for your interview with your heart pounding like your HIV test is about to come back positive. Then the robot-like guy behind the bulletproof glass will politely fire you with questions, 'Name, please?' 'Address, sir?' 'Nationality, ma'am?' 'Your documents?' 'Reason for travel?' 'Workplace?' 'Marital Status?', 'Duration of visit?'. Trying your best to put a good impression forward, you try light humor with a pinch of American accent and projecting a friendly and honest body language that the robot ignores along with eye contact. After successfully repeating the rehearsed lines a hundred times over without stuttering, on how you plan to study in America and how your family will pay for all your requirements, you show your I-something document and all have been processed. The Consular will nod, pretending to be studying your documents and finally tell you, "Sorry Sir, you are not the type of person we want in the United States of America, when you have a more solid reason to travel or you have a stronger family tie, please try again. Good day!" and they give you your receipt to hang on your wall at home, and also a red stamp in your passport as a token of your visit to the US Embassy, Nairobi. Stronger family tie? I have a mother, father and sister, what do you want me to do? Get married with children and then come back? If you object to the verdict, the polite robotic consular will tell you that it was according to some law or regulation, article this and paragraph that, indicated on the application form, section this, subsection that. As if the law was a nursery rhyme that everyone was familiar with. A rude consular officer will just zap you with her overworked eyes held together by an intricate web of red veins and at that very moment, you'll realize you hate all Americans because you were denied a visa to visit their God-given country and denied the opportunity to experience the American dream. Funny, but true! Shola believed Koto's theory after being denied a visa; though the consular was African American, she still felt there was a conspiracy to contain black people or maybe just Africans. The same conspiracy that made me lose Christie. There is the slight possibility though that the Consular guys just judge you by your clothes, your accent, and your face or maybe they just toss a dice or something.

"I think you have a problem. You need to grow up!" Boko concluded the visa discussion on that note, irritated, and I felt at peace since I got him back. It was satisfying seeing a nicely dressed guy with a funny haircut trying not to lose his cool.

"Sorry! Adult!" I chuckled.

Boko gave a long scrutinizing stare into me to find the real problem with his x-ray vision into my DNA and resigned with the type of look you give a confused child throwing a tantrum. Surprisingly, he still had the composure to ask when I started smoking. I did not feel inclined to explain why I had tobacco smell all over me. I went along with his assumption. I told him I had been smoking since Christie dumped me and I didn't know why I just do it. I told him the *devil* made me do it and he nodded as if he really believed it and looked as if he would pray for me.

The rest of my conversations on the flight with Boko was like a first date. Pauses, fiddling around with the gadgets in the seat, talk a little, read a little, then talk again. An Ethiopian lady sitting next to her husband in the row across the aisle behind the South African sniffed at everything. The tissue papers, lotions from her handbag, the seats; everything. It made me wonder what her zestless husband must have gone through. She was old and cranky; her husband looked exhausted. Behind the Ethiopian lady, a green-eyed woman patted the red hair of her freckled faced toddler who was fast asleep with his teddy as the pillow. A Cadbury chocolate and its wrappers smeared on his Barney T-shirt. The two Indian men in front of us smelled like onion and spices, they spoke in their native language the whole trip. The conversation was very lively and I felt like joining in, with their laughing and clapping at each other's remarks. Their intensity seemed to bother some of the other passengers at first, but tolerance prevailed, as many of the other passengers were chatting and those travelling alone shut their eyes, read the in-flight magazines, or got acquainted with their neighbours. The rest of the flight was like an ether-induced sleep, I saw nothing and felt nothing.

***

"Hope you enjoyed your flight, have a nice day", a tall hostess with a perfect fitting uniform and a graceful composure repeated after every passenger. Her teeth bright between dark gums; she politely smiled with the experience of hundreds of flight hours, not bothered by the indifference of some passengers who rarely noticed she was standing there. Customers are always hard to please.

Last summer, I was a shop attendant in a thatched roofed craft shop that smelt like bark cloth, straws and oil paint. We had loads of tourists in shorts from all over the world wanting to buy postcards, souvenir animals, key holders and sculptures of heavily endured half naked Masai people (mostly men). A pleasant looking lady in her late forties once came in with her husband of fifty-something; she said they were newlywed, but the husband looked depleted and was most likely thinking up an excuse for a divorce or unforeseen death. He had bags under his eyes and appeared slightly younger with his baseball cap tilted in a curve to the side, which was fashionable. He agreed with everything she said and stood to stare as she examined each souvenir like a priceless antique at the museum of natural history. After several inspections and studying of the crafts, she approached me like the guy from *the croc files*.

"Do you speak English?" she stretched the words slowly and used her hand to motion a slower gesture. Her hands motioned from her mouth to my direction.

"Yes, I do. I'm a student at the International School," I boasted with a warm customer-friendly smile. Her husband smiled delightfully too and he looked even younger as he approached me.

“Good! No Swahili?” She spoke with the deaf and mute in mind.

“A little.”

“Good for you. I am looking for the tall giraffe with the marble finishing, mounted on ebony,” she described with the aid of her hands, “it looks like this type of material,” she ran to a marble chessboard to touch a pawn.

“Please, do bear with us.”, Her husband murmured to me with a dimpled smile. I guess that was his way of warning me that his wife needed a lot of patience.

“I don’t think we have it.”

“You *think* or you don't have it?" she demanded with the authority of a headmistress as waves formed on her forehead.

“We don’t have it.”

“But I have a friend back home who got one from here. Isn’t this *Miss Jambo?*”

“This is *Miss Jambo*. It probably got sold out”

"You, don't seem to be sure. Can I speak to someone else who is sure?" She stared over me to the corner to Mrs Njoroge's sister who was supposed to be my boss and utilized every opportunity to declare it.

“The service here is poor, your boy doesn’t seem to know much about anything.” She addressed Nzeli. I felt like hitting her on the back of her head with my shoes for calling me a boy. A boy!

"I'm very sorry about that, you'll have to forgive us. His case has been forwarded to management several times. How can I be of service?" Nzeli responded in the phone American accent she acquired on a two-months visit to Naperville, Illinois. She made the craft shop sound like some multinational corporation. Management! Which management? "I am Nzeli, the manager." She introduced herself in her perky fluctuating octave voice and a business card.

“Yes, I am looking for a giraffe…”, she spoke as she handed Nzeli’s card to her husband, who in turn tucked it into his pocket without looking at it.

“The one mounted on ebony, marble finishing?” Nzeli interrupted.

“Yes, that one.”

“It’s a best seller! I just sold the last one forty-five minutes ago.” Nzeli lied, she probably heard the lady and lied about the giraffe. I never saw one that resembled it for the six weeks I worked at *Miss Jambo*.

"When do you hope to get the new supply?"

"In two weeks. The suppliers always delay because they are handcrafted"

"I know. Anyway, if we are here for that long, I'll be back for it."

"You are most welcome."

"Thank you my dear," the nag smiled to Nzeli and gave me a cold look. Her husband waved at me on their way out and I waved back. If Nzeli wasn't there, I probably would have gotten nasty for calling me a boy. Boy!

Every time Nzeli attended to a customer, she turned to me with the look that said 'incompetence'. On one occasion she told customers how incompetence strives in the country and seemed to point me out as one of the culprits. Ironically, she spent most of the time going for lunch or going to the 'bank'. She always showed up late to open the shop and always returned late to close up, which meant I had to wait beyond the closing time. Her excuse was always the incompetence perpetrated by the matatus or the 'bank'.

Koto told me that his great-grandmother was one of the wisest persons in their village before she died. The king himself would consult her whenever he needed advice on an important decision. She was known for her prophetic dreams and saw what ordinary human eyes could not see. Koto told about the festival of the red moon celebrated every third leap year, where the whole village would party till the next day, with no one allowed to sleep. She always spotted animals in human form walking upside down, restless ghosts walking backwards trying to retrace their steps and demons fondling young women in the fury of the fête. She was the one who discovered that the noises in the woods just before dawn were the lamenting scurry of the royal chief hunter's wife's ghost still searching for her late husband even in death, almost a quarter of a century after his disappearance and five years after her death. Moonlight tales by the flames of cooking pots on firewood revealed that the chief royal hunter was probably attacked by a wild animal. Till her death, his wife swore several times that she saw him by the woods, sometime standing still and other times walking into them with his spears, bow and arrows. She became obsessed with searching the woods for him and eventually the excessive grief pierced her to death. On her deathbed, she pleaded with her friends and relatives to continue searching for her husband. They all agreed with the full understanding that it was a mentally unstable person talking and left it at that.

When a problem was presented to her, Koto's great-grandmother would pause as though she was searching somewhere within her wrinkled body and after twenty minutes, sometimes hours, in silence she would give the best solution. By the time she concluded with her reasoning to the solution, the entire village council, including the King, would have their mouth wide open in awe. She would say her dreams confirmed every decision, sometimes before, other times after. Some believed she was too mysterious to be ordinary; she must be a witch, they cynically claimed since she had an answer to everything, but even witches don't know everything. Others declared that she had been to the Grand Fields of the Ancestors; she must have seen the complete mysteries of the universe, they claimed. She predicted the rebellion of the princes when they were only children, the great drought in a time of plenty, and the coming of foreign people. People mocked her and told her she was delirious, how could there ever be foreign people, since they knew all the neighbouring tribes and the neighbouring tribes knew their other neighbours. To them, nothing was foreign under the sun. Can the ancient eyes of the ancestor be thought to see anew?

If there are lands across lakes; there should be lands across seas she reasoned, it was confirmed in her dreams. The other elders of the village told her only the ancestors live across the seas, the Grand Fields of the Ancestors was across the seas, and if any went there, that meant the person was dead. She objected by telling them that if the Grand Fields existed and the people were supposed to be wise, then the dead would have returned to life. The elders agreed with this as villagers reported seeing the dead sometimes, on the way to the farm between early morning mists, late at night by the shadows poured out by the moon and in midnight slumbers dragging their heavy feet on shattered dreams. She objected still and that caused a lot of speculations and some elders said she was disrespectful to the ancestors. They said she was defying and challenging the ancestors by trying to belittle them with her old housewife rubbles. She had a dream. She said she saw God in the dream. He told her, he alone was God. She saw a wooden post with a transverse piece riddled with blood. She saw a baby in a manger. And she saw a majestic throne that words could not capture. Then she saw him. He was a man with hair whitened as wool by eternity. His face was radiant with youth, his voice thick with wisdom and his presence consoling to her, yet unapproachable! He called himself *the Ancient of Days.* She enquired which of her ancestor's spirit he was. What tribe he belonged to she demanded to know when he died. How old he was. All the questions came to her at once like a revelation. He said he was much older, wiser, and lived the span before the ancestors and beyond the future. She shared the dream with the elders in the king's council and they began to lose credibility in her and her wisdom. To them, the ancestors are gods and the king is their son and anyone who thinks otherwise was not meant to be an elder or alive.

Words of the white men's arrival in the coastal villages travelled like a folklore all the way inland to their village. Some say their complexion was bronze others said it was like the inside of the lightly roasted cocoa pod. Before long, they were described with several nonhuman attributes; they point fire, they bring the dead back to life, they change colour, they speak only incantations and they build their kingdom on the sea. When the King called for the elders, Koto's great-grandmother recommended that whatever gift the white men brought should not be accepted. It would be bait, she supposed. Self-confident elders wanted to go and attack the white men on their way from the coast, but news that the white men where both kind and extremely cruel demoralized them with perplexity. They resorted to calling on the ancestors to go and fight on their behalf, which did not happen.

When the white men finally came, they came with providence. The harvest that year had been bountiful like no other and that was a suggestion of a good omen. To top it all, they brought gifts and said they came in peace. They brought greetings from their King. Some of the white men were soldiers, some farmers and others claimed to be messengers of God, the God of heaven and earth, who created all things. It intrigued Koto's great-grandmother especially when they claimed their God was from before the beginning of time and goes beyond the end of time. He was older than days past and younger than the future to come. He is the beginning and the end. We all live, move and have our existence in this one God.

The new king of Koto's village, Satu, who was the rebellious son of the previous king, was overwhelmed; he accepted every one of their gifts. The young king, Satu, who had earlier led an insurrection against his father with the help of his brothers, killed and purged the whole village of anything that will remind them of their betrayed father. Rumours had it that the old King was buried alive with his personal guards, under the guise that he died in his sleep. A brief power struggle followed. The soil was dampened with the blood of their siblings, resisting chiefs, loyal guards, wives and concubines of the king with exceptions to their respective mothers. Years that followed the insurrection saw a fattened rift between the nobles and the peasants. Festivals were celebrated with what amounted to orgies and public display of financial temperament at the expense of the peasants who worked their bare backs. Forced to pay ever-increasing tributes of produce and merchandise to the king, their only hope was to die an early death. Satu's brothers were untouchable. They took whoever and whatever they wanted whenever they wanted it. It didn't get any better when one of them forced himself on Satu's favourite concubine. Satu had them all killed, along with their initially spared mothers and all his nephews and nieces. The royal bloodline must only run through one stream which leads to the ocean. The oceans that are Satu. Satu was from then on given the additional title of 'King of the oceans'. When the white men arrived from across the ocean, it seemed only right that the 'King of the oceans' gave them audience and indulged them.

The young monarch was astonished by his reflection in the mirror; the hair dye that made his mother younger, the music boxes and everything the white men possessed amused him. He was particularly interested in the rifles. He always told the white men to shoot his servants every now and then to admire the nature of the 'power', but they always preferred to shoot goats instead. King Satu completely disregarded the advice of the elders; especially Koto's great-grandmother whom he always thought was spared because of her wisdom which was beginning to echo folly. The ship he saw at the coast, its size and the realization that it was built by the white men overtook the king. They told him they had houses ten times the size of the village and they rose like a hill dressed in the beauty of flower gardens. They made lakes and mountains. They had many things back home that exceeded his wildest imagination. He called for a meeting with the elders and the chiefs of the village and told them he was planning to follow the white men to their country to see their magnificence. The weapons that could kill their enemies without shedding their own blood, the drink that made people lighter and what their king looked like all fed his curiosity. He wanted to personally create an alliance before other kingdoms did, with such strange and powerful people. It sounded like a good idea to the villagers as the rumour travelled through the market squares and rain drenched thatched roofs under heavy clouds on idle muddy afternoons. Koto's great-grandmother objected and the whole council did too. She argued that the village was the king's premier obligation. The sending of a delegation of chiefs was proposed. The king rejected.

The next day, the young lion: king Satu of Lalopukamala, conqueror of giants, husband of many, father of countless, son of the ancestors, grandson of the gods, fountain of goodness, master of the thousand villages, protector of virtues, installer of courage and more recently the king of the oceans, accused Koto's great-grandmother of forsaking the ancestors and wanting to worship the foreign gods. 'The young lion' lied that the ancestors came to him at night and told him so. Though the basis of the accusation germinated from a private conversation they had the day he took the throne. Satu in an attempt to win over Koto's great grandmother's support entertained the notion of there being a one true almighty God. He took it then as now, the ranting of an old and unbalanced woman who had influence in the villages. To disarm her of such great power, he had to throw doubt at her beliefs and judgment, thus making her the enemy. The perfect accusation was born! He also said that was why she had been objecting to the ancestors' will and did not believe in the Grand Fields. King Satu immediately ordered her to be killed. Nobody had the haughtiness to carry out his orders; they feared her because they respected her too much to dare. They feared the rumours about her, which were as diverse as the species in the bushes thickened by the darkness of the forest where souls are lost forever. Koto's great-grandmother walked out of the palace, her head searching the ground for answers, *they should have fed that child to the crocodiles when he was born*, she kept repeating. Everyone knew the young king was definitely lying, but since tradition says that 'the sons of the ancestors' can't lie, they all just had to follow his judgment or else they would be accused of objecting to the will of the ancestors too. Strangely 'the conqueror of giants' could not carry out his own orders himself. He just sat on the throne brimming with the infestation of hate and the prospect of possible retaliation from her or her supporters. Koto's great-grandmother left the village since no one was allowed to have any dealings with her or else they defy the king. She left the village in the silence and her absence was felt like a missing tooth in the mouth of a carnivore. She moved to the coast in search of a new life, one she found as a Christian with the enlightenment of white missionaries.

The king said he received a farsighted message that if Koto's great-grandmother were not cursed, the village society would be forsaken by the Ancestors and divine providence would be lost forever because the Ancestors were still angry with Koto's family. The village witch doctor was told to fashion a vile curse and set it off like a slingshot at Koto's family. The witch doctor cursed Koto's family that they would always be servants and they would all die a slow deteriorating death. Before she settled on the coast, Koto said his great-grandmother roamed from place to place with his grandfather and the rest of the family preaching the good news and working as farm-hands to make ends meet. Most of the people she shared her testimony with thought she was crazy or she was just a very convincing storyteller. She died on one of her missions along the coastal villages. They found her six days later; she died resting under a constellation of coconut trees with her sandals as her pillow. She was given a decent burial by the missionaries.

Satu, 'king of the oceans' left with the white men and it was a relief to the entire village. He took thirty-one of his young wives, seventy-one guards and twenty-one other officials and their families, making a total of a hundred-and-fifty-three people. The white men emphasized the need for healthy and able-bodied people since the trip would be treacherous and physically draining. The village was almost emptied of its vital populace.

***

We arrived at Entebbe International Airport and I went through the same questioning session with the Customs officers more than I had in Kenya with the same spectators. This time they were more interested in going through security before I did, and they all gave polite smiles as they passed by to meet their contacts in the arrival. The green-eyed lady met her husband and her son yelled 'daddy'. He fell down but did not cry and his father scooped him up with the chocolate on his Barney t-shirt and hugged his wife. I couldn't find the South African lady and her travelling companion, I assumed they were in transit. The two Indians were met by a large group of Indians and hugs and back patting sounded. Boko waited for me to go through; he was flagged to go through without problems.

Kintu was a former schoolmate at the International British School in Kenya. He was also fresher in Global University Kampala and he helped us with most of the paperwork in the admission process. We had been classmates through high school in Kenya. We were in the same class all the way to the 11th grade. His father was initially a diplomat in Kenya. The summer break before the 12th grade he went to Spain for vacation and his parents divorced before he returned. He moved with his mother back to Uganda, while his father went off to a new posting in Thailand with a new Kenyan girlfriend, one-third of his age. Kintu introduced me to my first bottle of beer and then my first vodka because he said it would make Christie jealous when she saw I was having fun without her. That night at the Carnivore, I got drunk and slept over at his place with a guilty feeling panging at my conscience, a feeling that lasted almost a week.

Ever since Kintu made his first trips in the 9th grade to the US, UK, and Jamaica, he would do anything to pass for an African American, or someone from anywhere else but Africa. He wore baggy designer jeans, sagging to reveal his Calvin Klein cotton boxers and his shoes always looked brand new. The Nike T-shirt he was wearing was partially tucked into his boxers and his dreadlocks sparked like the surface of a pool on a sunny afternoon. If it wasn't a brand name, you probably won't find it on Kintu. The truth is that his mother probably did not trust him living abroad alone. He was her baby.

He liked to look lean and mean, like a gangster he claimed. His nose, ears and eyebrows were pierced. He wanted to be a rapper, dreamt of winning a Grammy and wanted to study business to enable him manage his talent. His mother could not afford an education in the US, as his father originally promised.

"Sup my Niggas?" the clear American accent pronounced as he approached us, bouncing to the tune of his clapping silver chains. He had an iPhone in his hand and his baseball cap tucked in his front jeans pocket. I hugged him and he gave Boko a weak handshake with an identical smile like the one he gave me. Like compatriots meeting in a foreign land, they never got along in high school, but they seemed to have mutual respect for each other.

"My Niggas lets go party!" He yelled into Boko's left ear as he turned round to leave the arrival launch, with his jeans falling. This caught everybody's attention and some laughed while others just ignored it. He didn't bother helping us with our bags; he just waved us to follow him, walking like his legs were uneven.

Two girls waited in his car dressed in brightly colored outfits like backup dancers in a hip-hop music video. The one originally in the front passenger seat with a brazen face hopped into the back seat while we forced our bags into the car's trunk. Boko beat me to the front seat and gave an embellish look as we were introduced to the ladies in the 'lipstick' red Toyota Corolla as Kintu called it. Lydia was Kintu's girlfriend, a second-year law student who would easily pass for a porn star. Lydia's friend, Helen, she was more of the Lenin in *Of Mice and Men.* They were more like conjoined twins, the way they giggled and chuckled at every gesture we made. I wondered if they would laugh if I farted, but I didn't. I tried chatting with Lydia, being my friend's girl. She loved Grisham's novels and drooled at the charm, intelligence, and strategies of the lawyers in them. I told her about my interest in law in the 9th grade after watching the whole first season of Boston Legal, how it lasted for a week. I didn't tell her I toyed with the idea of being a porn star before that and she would have made a great co-star. Both Lydia and Helen giggled through my chat as though everything I said was funny. To me, it was a sign that they were stupid. Boko indulged in asking statistical and demographic questions about Uganda; the population growth rate, GDP, infant mortality, rural-urban migration, export and import and the works. To my surprise, Kintu answered all his questions and gave additional facts about his country and its role in the region. Kintu pointed out that Ugandan troops are keeping the peace in Somalia. Peace in Somalia? It made me laugh. The thought of Kintu being so formal was out of character.

At first, I thought they were giggling at each other's girl talk, but it became irritating and I couldn't help but ask Kintu if the girls were living next to us by any chance because I would have to buy ear-plugs. He said no. Boko turned back, looked at me and smiled. The girls seemed upset by my question, their giggling stopped for a while, but after we drove a few kilometres, they started again. Kintu offered Boko a can of beer, he turned it down and it was passed on to me. The ladies shared one and Kintu drank the third. Boko asked if drinking and driving in Uganda was legal and Kintu brushed him off with a long blank stare for someone driving that made me nervous.

Jay-Z was on the radio, then Eminem, after that I lost track. Helen was either revealing her upper thighs or her skirt was just having a hard time concealing them. She was sitting on my lap, or maybe it had something to do with her huge hips. It seemed she wiggled with the motion of the waist of a belly dancer, so coy and graceful that I tried so hard not to attach too much to it. My attempts were futile, my mind had already gone to places where I would never dare to let my mother know. Just by looking at her, I tried to think of something distant from Helen's lap, but it was hard. Lydia seemed lost in her mobile phone as the clicking of text could be heard.

Kintu tried initiating conversation with Boko again, but Boko was more absorbed by the scenery we were driving through. The hills, the trees, the new estates bright among the coarse green trees, and tattered roadside kiosks decorated with fruits and crafts. Kintu stared through the rear-view mirror to see what I was up to, but I pretended to be absorbed into the scenery too. Kintu changed the song back to Jay-Z and then Eminem again.

The way the houses became sparse as we drove away from Entebbe, and how the houses also began to take the forms of clay and mud seemed poetic to me. An international airport and a few miles away, people who have never seen and will never see the interior of a plane. A pregnant woman was standing on the roadside waiting for a taxi. I wondered if she was happy with her life, her husband and her child to be. She looked exhausted and in deep thought from the glimpse I got of her in a dark brown dress that seemed heavy on her. I was always curious what it would be like being somebody else, why they deserve to be who they are and not me. If we are really all unique as my mother claims, if some are more important than others as my father complains and if some are just unlucky or cursed as Koto would put it. I wondered if there was anybody in the world out there who feels like I do, trapped in something and not knowing what exactly it is. Just knowing I am in prison for a crime I don't know I have committed and wishing to walk away from everything…everything…into the trees maybe, or into the air like I craved at Point Lenana.

Acacia trees, grass and farms that covered the hills gave me the sense of what Koto's village might have looked like with the exclusion of the TV antennas. The trees waved their branches dancing to an ancient African spiritual I could not hear. Bush paths wiggled their way through the grass and under the trees, like endless journeys that fade to the peak of the hills and in the valleys. I saw women and older children carrying firewood, clay pots and other items on their heads with their toddlers following as chicks follow the hen, finding their way through the bush paths to their houses where happiness or sorrow awaits. Men cycling along the road on bicycles of various histories carried wives, children, large pieces of furniture, a bunch of bananas, and any other thing demanded by their predicaments. Some looked happy, some sad, most just had blank faces like a calm lake on a windless night, never knowing what is beneath.

The traffic built up as we approached Kampala. A dusty temple being painted by a clock tower roundabout dedicated by the Queen reminded me of the two Indians on the flight, their laughing and clapping. Another temple in the distance with elaborate finishing peeped on a slope next to a Shell station. Kintu said only one was a Hindu temple and that the other was some sort of religion.

The traffic was heavy, selfish drivers building more commotion. Four-wheel drives and minivans with blue dotted stripes roared off on the pavements in their attempts to avoid the jam at the roundabout. Some of the policemen standing by stared the other way as if they did not see, while the aggressive drivers drove others mad. Kintu stared out the window as though he was looking for someone and stretched his arm out the window to indicate he was turning right. I wondered why he was not using his indicators. None of the drivers next to him paid attention to his gesture, but he forcefully changed lane and nearly got hit by several motorcyclists. The motorcyclists yelled in Luganda while their helmetless passengers nodded with disapproval. Kintu pointed his middle finger and drove into the approaching lane, causing traffic congestion on the lane that had been flowing smoothly. There was shouting and swear words falling out as we drove past cars in the other lanes. Boko was nodding his head in total disapproval and I was just praying that we didn't get killed or arrested. The girls were chatting about the Latin American soap *Second Chance*. They both felt, Salvador, the main character who returned from the dead as a shirtless underwear model, should not forgive one of the other characters.

"Kintu, you don't need to impress us. You are a good driver!" Boko consoled in his mature approach. The girls yelled out laughing and I felt irritated enough to jump out of the car and walk.

"This is Kampala!" Kintu replied without looking at Boko. He sounded really tough when he said it like it was nothing. Boko nodded in disapproval again and turned his face to the window.

"Don't get us killed, Action Hero!" Boko said staring out the window.

"Whatever!" Kintu grumbled and the girls laughed out louder. I could see their laughter was upsetting Boko as well, but he just ignored them. I turned my face to the window by my side and it seemed Helen tugged at me with her hip deliberately this time, but I ignored her and she giggled like a witch in a car on a Friday afternoon.

"Hey, Kintu slow down" I intervened. Trying to take charge of the situation.

"Chill, dude. Don't freak out" was Kintu's response as we returned to our lane after passing the congestion. The thought of a kid who died in a car crash when we were in the 11th grade troubled me. I did not want to end up like Darren. He was with some friends when it happened. They were over speeding and rammed into the back of a petrol tanker. The driver and the other two boys in the car came out with no visible injury, but poor Darren Owerri was pinned under the dashboard which was buried under the tanker. We had a memorial for him at school and his mother was inconsolable, she looked like a woman broken into a million pieces. The story was all over the media, they said he died on the spot. Darren's remains were plastered all over the newspapers. One had his lifeless body under the shattered windshield, his hand clenched in a fist rested on the dashboard. His brother sat right behind him in the car and saw his big brother's lifeless body. Some bystanders tried to help Darren out of the car, while others took pictures. His brother stood there like a lifeless form in shock, not moving, not talking. He just had tears rolling down his porcelain face.

We stopped by a Food Court, Boko had chips and fish fillet, the girls shared a pizza, Kintu settled for curry rice and chicken, I had mushroom steak and mashed potatoes. We all took orange juice. Opposite the Food Court, Kintu showed me a building my father's firm designed; it looked better than the pictures I saw. Boko teased Kintu about running for Mayor of Kampala since he knew almost everybody in the Food Court. He waved and gave hugs at intervals as a result of people waving to him or coming to our table to say 'hello'. After using the restroom, I returned to find Kintu was trying to stop the road service guys from clamping his car. Though he parked in the right slot, he had not paid several of his parking tickets. He gave them 'something' and he was told to go to their head office in Nakasero to clear his parking ticket fines or his car would be towed away next time. We passed by the ATM, then Nakasero to pay for the parking tickets and the fine. We also passed by the university to get forms to register in our departments. It was Friday, and the secretaries behind their government assigned typewriters told us to come back on Monday. The registration forms were 'over' they said in both the medical school and the ICT building. We were ignored after that. We drove around campus, Kintu was supposed to meet someone at the university bookshop, but the person was gone, we came an hour late. He called and the guy said 'tomorrow' or Monday.

Our apartment was located in Ntinda, close to lots of bars and takeaways, which really proved Kintu chose the house. He said it was the only one he could get in our price range. It backed a slum that spread out into the valley with dusty roads running through it like a faded rug. The air always smelled of roasted pork, chips and a collage of rotten odours oozing from the garbage. In the building, there were two internet cafes downstairs, a hairdressing salon and a tiny supermarket that was more of a passageway. It wasn't what I had expected initially, but Boko said we should give it a try. Like I had a choice. The interior made me change my mind though; it was neat and nicely furnished with lively colours. It was a three-bedroom flat with a kitchen, store, two bathrooms, and a huge living room. The potpourri waffled a lavender fragrance; the television was a Sony, and an ash grey leather sofa set sat beneath a matching rug under the balsa-wood centre table.

"Now we're talking, this place is nice," I had to confess savouring the pictures on the wall.

"My mom did it," Kintu admitted, stealing a glance at his watch.

"She's very good!" Boko complimented, his suitcase leaning on the single sofa.

"Thanks!" Kintu acknowledged. The girls helped with my suitcase, I had my backpack on and Kintu had one of Boko's hand luggage, which he dropped on the three-sitter. Kintu's mother owned a large furniture shop on Acacia drive in a posh part of town. She had the same business in Kenya but moved to Uganda after the divorce. Her business partner, a tall model like middle-aged Eritrean took over. My initial suspicion was that she caused the divorce, but I was wrong.

I had the room next to Kintu's cubical with a wide window that overlooked the rusty iron sheets of the shanty houses. Farther away, there was a green hill with brown tiled roofs dispersed on it. Boko's room was on the other side of the passage, next to the bathroom we shared. It was bigger and rectangular in shape, with wide windows that faced the neighbouring house. All the rooms had wardrobes with dressing mirrors on their doors. Kintu had the self-contained master bedroom, his own bathroom and two wide windows; one facing the slums, the other facing the neighbours. The girls watched a movie while we tried to get ourselves sorted out. They watched a Nigerian movie about an evil stepmother who bewitched her stepdaughter. It was the usual infidelity, evil stepmothers, witchcraft, pastors, lots of crying and finally the bad guys all died before the movie ended, the unfaithful husband asks his wife's forgiveness and they started their life afresh. Or better yet, wait for part two to see the very end. The girls loved it and they cried along with the movie. We made fun of them. They called us heartless.

After settling in, Kintu's mother invited us for dinner at her place in Muyenga where she stayed with a maid, a gateman and a toy boy Kintu could not stand. Kintu said he always had to ‘swallow his own vomit' when he saw his mother kissing the catfish lookalike boyfriend she was dating, probably to infuriate his father. Kintu would have accused the catfish of being a gigolo, but he was probably fifteen years younger than his mother and he inherited a huge bank account from his late father's business prowess. The catfish always tried to act older while Kintu's mother tried to act younger and this really pissed Kintu off. She agreed openheartedly when Kintu came up with the idea of moving out and staying with his friends. She said it would help him become independent, but she paid all the bills. Kintu claimed they probably run around the house naked since they can't keep their hands off each other especially now that he finally left home. He accused his mother of not acting like an African and we all laughed. The sarcasm!

Boko and I called our parents informing them of our safe arrival. My mother told me to send her regards to Kintu's mother. They were good friends back in Kenya and did a lot of shopping and exchanged notes on marriage life which seemed not to have yielded much. She also asked if I was 'ok' about five times and told me to make sure I call at least once a week to make sure that all was going well. She cried on the phone about my father and me for a while and how he was coming on business. That made me feel weird. I did not know what to tell her. I just listened and kept telling her, "I am ok, mommy. It's Ok", that was all I could sum up to console her. She told me Mrs. Njoroge had been admitted to the hospital and might not make it. She cried some more. I wasn't sure if she was crying for me, Mrs. Njoroge or something else. She said my father sent his love; I sent mine back too. It was a relief to hang up. Though I knew my father was meant to come to Uganda. I deliberately made sure we did not come on the same day. The thought of me seated next to him in a concealed place like an airplane meant we would have to talk. I had nothing to say to him. Most of what he would say I probably would not be interested in hearing.

We drove through Kampala and had something to eat again at a takeaway restaurant in Wandegeya. We dropped the girls off at their hostel. Lydia invited us in, but Kintu said he was in a hurry. We went to shops and offices where Kintu introduced us to his female friends of various sorts; some exes, others just clubbing buddies. I envied the way he was able to humour them with a word, a touch or a simple gesture. They all found him hilarious and definitely cute. Boko sat in the background most of the time fading away into the setting along with the flower pots and soft boards. I tried to join the conversation, but always seemed to hit the wrong notes. My voice even sounded awkward to my own ears.

While I was working for Mrs. Njoroge at *Miss Jambo*, I tried being smooth with Nzeli, but it was always bumpy. Always helping her pick things up and letting her go through the door first, hoping she'd notice the nice guy I was, but she only acknowledged I was a good subordinate. When I told her I was interested in her over a late lunch I sponsored on payday, she said I was not her type. Too young, too inexperienced, too dependent and the list went on. She concluded with a threat that she *eats clumsy guys like me for snack.* I was strongly convicted she got the line from a movie, but it scared me anyway. Her dark mascara and lipstick made her look like a black widow spider. I had the image of her chewing my arms and legs the way she did the Buffalo wings. She didn't ease the rejection by offering we should be friends; she ate the free lunch I bought her and told me not to be late to work the next day. I hated her from then on.

***

We loitered around Garden City, spotted pretty girls, had ice cream and checked what movie was showing that night. At the end of our tour, Boko asked if there was any church that Kintu could recommend. Kintu paused for a while as if he was really searching the back of his mind, and told him there was St. Matthews on campus. Boko said he was Pentecostal. "What's the difference?" Kintu seemed to want to ask.

"You can try KFC...Just teasing, KPC," he finally said reluctantly.

Kintu told him: "they have good music and pretty girls." Kintu said he used to attend the church when there was a *saved* girl he developed an interest in.

"It is always about girls with you," Boko responded pulling the newspaper from me without asking if I was still reading it.

"So, are you saved?" Kintu asked Boko who was in the back seat of the car partially reading the newspaper.

"Yes," he admitted.

"That's why you didn't take the beer?" He questioned while smiling at me.

"Yap!" Boko answered not looking up from the newspaper. Kintu and I chuckled, while a 2Face track rapped on the car music system.

"Jesus made wine in the bible, at the wedding party," Kintu preached, "and wine is alcohol if I'm not mistaken."

"I heard the same!" Boko replied sarcastically without a twitch. We laughed out loud and Boko joined in.

"This is Jay-Z's last tour recording," Kintu informed as the next song began.

"That explains why it's been playing the whole day," I remarked, having heard the same song earlier.

"Ya. *Jigga my nigga,*" he almost whispered to himself, "I'm gonna miss those lyrics."

"Is he dead?" Boko asked from the back, but we both ignored

him.

"Kintu, what happened with the saved girl?" I banally asked.

Kintu met her at a Takeaway restaurant in Wandegeya, he approached her, and she said she was only interested in a relationship that would lead to marriage. He said it as though that was her first remark when he said 'hello'. Kintu tried to impress her by attending church services with her to project an image of responsibility and spirituality both of which he had in minute quantities. He would spend the whole service staring at her singing in the choir and fantasizing the possibilities of what he could do with her curves. To his disappointment, she was more in love with Jesus than she would ever be with any man. After trying everything in the book, he managed to get her to the movies, but she came with a whole group of guys whom he said were all hyper and tried to act cool. The exact word was 'sugar high group' who hopped and leapt like they were on something illegal. The movie was *The Passion* and it was the longest movie he ever watched. She sobbed saying, 'see what he has done for us.' When he asked who, she replied, 'Jesus.' He tried consoling her by stealing a hug or embrace, but it all felt awkward. The thought of Jesus dying for 'our' sins and trying to make out seemed at odds with each other.

The *saved* girl from KPC called him up one evening at around 9 p.m. and asked if he wanted to hang out with her. The exciting thought ran through his head like a nude lady. The gentleman approach he adopted for the last few weeks was about to pay dividends, he thought. He thought that would be the day he would claim his reward. He bought a pack of imported condoms, new boxers and even shaved his armpits. To his astonishment, she took him to an overnight prayer meeting. He was disgusted. A friend called him up at about midnight, asking why he wasn't at the TFI night at the Club. He used the excuse to lie that there was an emergency. He ran out of that church like it was really an emergency and she said she would be praying that 'God takes control'. He ran like a bat out of hell, he ran like a naked man looking for at least a modest mean of restoring his dignity and instil modesty. He ran like a vampire from the piercing sun. To find his fix elsewhere; he ran. Kintu said he was not sure if she meant 'control' of the emergency or control of him. After that incident, he had never set eyes on her again. He made sure he avoided her. Whenever she called his mobile, he didn't pick it up or told someone else to answer it and tell her that he travelled to the UK.

The story cracked me up and I could not stop laughing. It made Kintu so upset that he had to tell me it wasn't funny because the girl played with his sensitive emotions.

“For real, I would've married the girl!” He tried to make us sympathize with him.

"Would your mother allow you?"

"Of course!"

“But why didn’t you?”

“She didn't wanna give me some love!” He stated.

“Do you have to have sex to show love?” Boko asked imitating his voice sarcastically. He stared at Boko as if Boko was far beyond stupid. Boko smacked him lightly on the head with the newspaper.

“Don’t start that B.S. about no sex before marriage thing with me. Don’t you read the news? What if she is a she-male? You want me to discover that on my wedding night? Uh?” He asked with a sincere look on his face and with an anticipated response from Boko. My belly ached with laughter.

“And do you mean to tell me you ain’t never had some good old sex before? Give me a break, you can use that line on your moms, not on me. I know!” He scowled.

“Well, it depends on your mind…”

"Whatever!" Kintu interrupted him and turned to me, "don't lie to me that you have never got laid too? Boko might be a weird freak, but you…"

“Guys, I am not interested in the topic, can’t you guys find something more decent to talk about?” I tried to change the discussion.

"I thought you're the one laughing; now you wanna be decent!" Kintu rolled his eyes as though he was upset, but stole the opportunity to take a glimpse of a lady in a mini hot pink outfit on the pavement.

Down Kampala Road, we were pulled over by traffic officers. The two police officers approached the car; one had a round belly with his trousers almost falling in the face of his flat behind, the other was extremely skinny and she seemed to be wearing her father's uniform.

“Hello boss, did you notice you just drove out of a one way which is not an exit?”

"I did not know Afande. I am very sorry. I'm just getting used to the new road plans. I just arrived from abroad today." Kintu lied politely to complement his lie. The policemen beamed and asked if his travel was fruitful. The officer was kind enough to inquire how the weather was treating us and Kintu in particular. He spoke as though they were old friends.

"Do you know that your third party has expired since yesterday?" The skinny officer declared by interrupting the friendly conversation. Her voice was assertive and her face was quite hostile, as though the weather had not been kind to her.

"Yea, yes madam", Kintu replied in an understanding and almost meek tone, "I was just on my way to renew it", he lied again.

"But you can buy from any petrol station," the fat friendly officer stated, gesturing the vastness of petrol stations with his right hand.

"That is one! Okay, let me see your driving permit." The skinny officer demanded. Kintu quickly passed it through the lowered tinted window. She snapped it from his hand without making any eye contact like a disgruntled ex-lover.

"Ehm Chief, do you know that your third-party expired and you are driving recklessly on the road, compromising road safety and your passengers' lives?" The skinny police officer asserted as she handed the permit back. Still without making eye contact. Her eyes were scanning the car from headlights to rear bumper for any form of other violations she could add to the list. The fat police officer walked around the car looking for a flaw in a more casual matter than his colleague. Kintu pulled out a ten thousand shillings note from his noisy yellow Velcro denim wallet and handed it to the skinny police officer, but the fat one intercepted it. He acted like he was about to uphold the law, but his intent proved otherwise.

"Big boss, for a Friday, this is small." The fat policeman stated as he handed his empty hat into the car where the sound of Velcro yielded a twenty thousand shilling note that was dropped in.

"I think you should check the pressure on your back tyres," the skinny office advised, while the bigger one waved us off.

***

We passed by a friend of Kintu's mother, Madam Neema. She had a new Barbing Salon; she was extremely proud of and she professed in as the jewel in her crown. She was a pleasant lady with a face riddled with confident smiles and heavy makeup. She spoke with Boko in French and a native Congolese language and tried to find out the last time he was in the DRC. Nine years ago, the war made it impossible to go back. She knew his family; they were once the biggest diamond dealers in Congo. They had their own mine, but Mobutu, the former dictator sent them off and the war kept them away. His father now runs a trucking company that transports food for the UN agencies, NGOs and other businesses that need heavy commodities moved into the ravaged war zone. Most of his employees, like madam Neema's, are Congolese, with bleached skin, excessive gold chains and a unique sense of colourful impeccable fashion.

"Young men, this is the innovative pioneering saloon for the gents of the millennium", Madam Neema's francophone accent forced out of her fat bleached neck, like a dry cough. Choker chains and all sorts of jewellery dangled from her stout body, hidden by the elaborate African attire she had on. Congolese music flocked the saloon that smelled like an overpriced aftershave.

"We can make different hairstyles, every hairstyle", she stated, "you can buy anything you need here." She continued as she pointed at the narrow corridor leading to what looks like an alley.

"For real?" Kintu emphasized, fascinated by the space management.

"We have beers and sodas on sale in the evenings with pretty campus girls and queen dancers on the weekends", she advertised.

"It's a barbing saloon and a bar?" Kintu clarified in amazement.

"Yes. And more. That is why I called it 'Multipurpose,'" she declared proudly.

Madam Neema's *Multipurpose* had shoes, jewellery, car air fresheners, computer accessories, mobile phones, snacks and other diverse items on sale. It was a one-stop Barbing Saloon. I could do all my shopping while having my haircut and lunch at the same time. 'Hair and there' should be their motto! We hung around in her shop for a while. Some new business ideas came to her it seemed; she wanted my mother to supply her with West African clothing and materials to sell in Kampala. I brushed the idea off. Boko had a trim; Kintu and I bought gold-plated rings we probably would never use. Kintu paid for everything. Boko and I got some money changed at the Forex Bureau next door. We planned to open a bank account the next day.

***

Kigundu, the catfish that is Kintu's mother's *toy boy*, looked five years older than I was. He had an overgrown beard and tried to remind us how young we were the whole evening. Kintu ignored him, on several attempts to be funny. He laughed at his own jokes! He was truly an audience of one.

"When I was on campus, things were so different", Kigundu in a lovelorn face said to Kintu's direction, "that was way back."

"Never knew you went to university, always thought you were a dropout," Kintu said fiddling with his vegetables as his jaw bones vibrated with anger. Boko stared at me and I stared back. Kintu's mother frowned in her son's direction. His voice was fuelled by composed rage on the brink of spilling over. Kintu deliberately chose his words with carelessness hoping that one of them would wound the playboy who now thinks himself a father. Worst yet his father.

"You are so funny, Kintu, I like your humour...I dropped out to make my fortune," Kigundu tried to laugh the remark away and deliberately sounded cocky to ignite Kintu's rage.

"Yeah, whatever," Kintu whispered with the breath of a furious dragon. I was staring hard at my food to avoid bursting out into laughter that would leave me rolling on the floor. It was more likely if I made just one more eye contact with Boko. I assumed Boko felt the same way too. Kintu had a strict face; he looked like a hardboiled egg on the brink of cracking. The room was suddenly filled with an awkward silence; the type you find in a room filled with total strangers with nothing in common. It seemed everybody wished time would stop being so sluggish because one way or the other we all did a time check. Kintu's mother looked at the wood grain wall clock as though she just remembered something and was not really looking at the time. Her young lover threw his hand weighted down by a Patek Philippe gold watch on the table and tilted it till its dial glowed on his face. The same watch he had told me earlier could buy his BMW. Kigundu's arch-rival asked me for the time the same way you would ask the concierge just before checking out. It was more of a reminder than a request, to which Boko gave a look which I understood as 'it's getting late' or at the very least 'let's get out of here'.

"Mom, my third party expired, can you help me out?" The awkwardness was silenced with a request.

"When did it expire?"

"I'll have to check."

"Come and pick it at the office tomorrow, but don't you think it's about time you learn how to renew it yourself?" She said beaming at Kiggundu who was nodding in absolute agreement. His gaze ended on Kintu, emphasising the point of maturity. Kintu showed composure and met his gaze coldly with an undertone of hostility. Kintu returned to the vegetables on his butter-coloured ceramic plate pretending like he didn't hear what the catfish had nonverbally communicated.

"Just go to any petrol station with your log book,", Kiggundu added with a self-righteous tone that was specially designed to provoke Kintu. Kintu showed maturity and composure by not responding but the vibrations in his jaw bones could almost be heard and definitely seen. The thought of Kintu stabbing Kiggundu with the fork in his humming hand did not seem too farfetched.

"You lads are very quiet," Mrs Nalubega, Kintu's mother said, aiming the statement at Boko and I. Her wide smile made me realise she looked more like a Kikuyu and would make a decent cover for a cookbook, but not Vogue. The clear accent with a hint of British education and the posture of a royal might have been a factor in Kiggundu's interest. It could also be the fact that she caught her ex-husband with his girlfriend in their marital bed and she was composed and polite enough to tell the girl to get dressed. She gave the girl 500 Kenya shillings (for services rendered) and the bed covers on which the dirty deed had taken place. She sternly asked her husband who was profusely apologising to escort the girl home. Her husband was so perplexed, he thought it wise not to sleep in the same house to eliminate the fear that she might possibly stab him to death in his sleep. His fear snowballed into the phobia that she had something up her sleeves and she was just waiting for the right time to execute it. Even after they divorced, that same fear lingered with him; the thought of a woman not showing anger whatsoever after such a discovery was almost diabolical to him. Every now and then when things went wrong at work or a freak occurrence happened around him, the face of his ex-wife was the first that rang in his mind and the possibility of her being the cause of such an occurrence. In fact, in the last few years since they separated, he was believed to be constantly haunted by the nagging feeling that his ex-wife, Kintu's mother, was bewitching him. Though he had no proof and her gesture even after the divorce had always been cordial, the thought of not being as potent in bedroom affairs was attributed to her.

"We're just enjoying the tasty meal," Boko answered for both of us like a commercial. I agreed quickly with a smile of satisfaction merged with a nod. We spoke about my family, Boko's and the condition back in Kenya. Kintu left the table first stumping into the corridor; Kigundu made him lose his appetite with his unspoken declaration. Kigundu left after that, since Kintu made him upset too, but tried very hard to conceal his hurt. Kintu ultimately settled for the TV and Kigundu went outside to his new BMW Z3 convertible. Mrs Nalubega apologised for their behaviour and we responded like it was nothing. I even tried to argue that it was a sign of a normal healthy family, to which Boko gave me a slap on the head with his stare. We spoke about Uganda and had more grilled pork, rice, matooke, groundnut sauce and peas. We left Mrs Nalubega's place at about eleven after she gave her son a lecture on manners. She called him to the kitchen and spoke in the same calm, but firm tone that she probably used on her ex-husband. Kintu sulked for the rest of the evening; his head hung low like a nursery school kid having a timeout. While his eyes appeared to squint, his lower lip seemed to do the opposite by appearing more pronounced. We waved 'bye' to Kigundu in the compound as he fondled his car and gave the gateman instructions on how to clean it. Kintu did not waste time on him.

Got home at eleven-forty, the bars in the neighbourhood were in full swing with band music playing. Kintu and Boko watched TV; I went to bed.

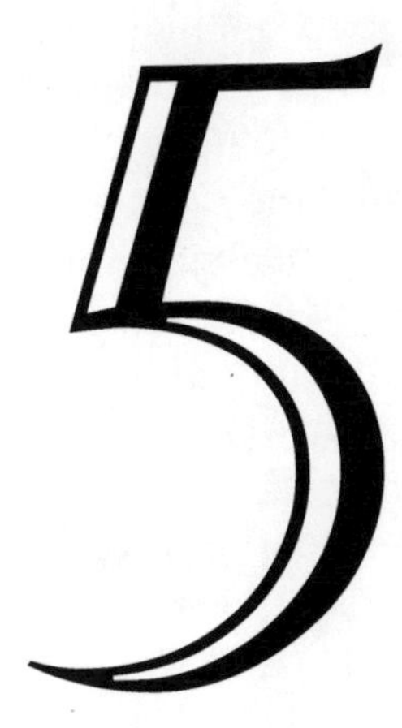

I had a frightening dream: running in a dark place, terrified, running from something in the darkness to the darkness, not knowing where to go, but still running aimlessly. A drowning sensation choking me, my feet working like on a treadmill, with motion, no movement. My entire body was heavy and though I used all my effort to run, I wasn't moving fast enough. I was barely walking. Though within me, all my efforts were poised at running. Then I started to sink. I realized I was running away from my father and running to him, but he was swallowed up by something more frightening, and terrifying. Screaming my head off, I wanted to wake up. It came closer. I was sinking. It's sucking me in. I was dying. I didn't want to dream anymore. I wanted to wake up.

I woke up. I was covered in beads of sweat. I wasn't sure if the dimly lit room was part of the terrifying dream or if it was just morphed into the dream to pull me back into reality. It was the latter.

My watch glowed four-fifty-six. I had the dream again. The dream of me feverishly running away from something. The dream that had haunted me for the last four years it seemed and had been intensifying in recent years. My mother said it had to mean something, something to do with my fears. Koto said it could be demons. Since the day his diagnosis rolled off his charred lips into a vast cultural gala in my head, it has lingered there like a childhood nursery rhyme that simply refuses to be forgotten.

Before, it was just the darkness, the drowning, the sinking and the running; since my father's confession, I started seeing him in the dreams too. I am not sure if he was the demon or the one that kept the demon at bay.

On my way to the sitting room, a cockroach darted under the toilet door, it frightened me. I had to swallow hard to make sure my heart did not pop out of my mouth. Though my reaction was an over exaggeration, I felt it was necessary after such a dream. Kintu had music playing in his room, the music outside was dead. There where dogs barking far away and isolated laughter from the slums by the window where tinted lights seemed to flicker on and off across the scattered shanty. I watched part of a movie on Mnet, about a serial killer who woke up at midnight to chop up his victims and woke up in the morning without a clue of what he did in the dark the night before. On Discovery channel, it was ghost night. I did not watch it for long, it was the last thing I needed. There was an interview on the local channel, a guy who became famous overnight but hated his fame, although wanted to go into movies, maybe music and perhaps books in the future. On a local Christian channel, a pastor in an oversized suede suit declared every moment as appointed by God; everything happened for a precise purpose to achieve the greater good. He gestured while claiming that the viewers were not watching by mistake and God was trying to talk to somebody. It made me look around the dull room, with lights from the verandah peeping through the curtains. I switched off the TV and went back to sleep.

***

Madam Shuweta and her husband lived in the only flat on the ground floor where her garden seemed to be competing for space with the shops next to her. Her husband worked with an Indian-owned computer retail store and Kintu was trying to get a laptop through him. It had not materialized for the last two weeks since he moved in. On the top floor, there was a lawyer with a large and noisy family, and in the opposite apartment was a spinster, Kintu accused of being a prostitute, because she always came back late with different men, mostly white. The flat opposite ours was unoccupied to the best of my knowledge, but it had curtains on the window.

***

I woke up at nine when Boko knocked to inform me breakfast was ready—a gesture of his magnanimous nature as his conceited face communicated unknowingly. A forgotten relief hopped over me, realizing the fact that I dreaded cooking and someone had come to my rescue. Boko made us boiled eggs, sausages and bread, which he sent the security man for from the narrow supermarket he guarded downstairs. We watched a movie on Mnet that Kintu had been dying to see. It had a lot of karate and I could not make out the star as it seemed they all died at the end. He said there was a part two and I wondered if their ghosts came back to life or they kept fighting in heaven or hell, whichever.

We made it to the bank in time and filled out forms, made photocopies of our passports, four passport-size photographs we took earlier in the day and our initial deposits of 200,000 Uganda shillings. By one o'clock, the elf-looking lady attending to us summarized by ordering us to claim our ATM cards on Wednesday afternoon. She looked eager to get us out of the bank since the closing was at noon and we had been pestering her since 11 o'clock. I asked what time, but she retorted, 'any time,' and walked off quickly as though trying to avoid any other question we might have.

Lydia met us at Gabba beach and disappeared with Kintu for almost two hours. Boko and I had fried fish, and played soccer with a Christian youth group we met there. They paid more attention to Boko than they did to me. Boko said I was paranoid again. On our way home, we dropped Lydia at a friend's wedding, she invited us to come along, but Kintu refused, so we stuck with him.

In Garden city, I called Christie. Her parents said she was out with a friend. I called Shola; the phone rang for a while and she finally picked up when I was about to give up. Her voice drained and echoed with the sadness of a coffee-drunk blues singer, hiding an irritated sting that could be sensed in her cool and almost coldly indifferent voice.

"I told you to stop calling!" She snapped on the phone and I could almost smell alcohol in her raspy voice. Probably the combination of coffee, whiskey and milk, she claimed she invented

"What? This is Tola", she laughed for almost ten seconds and I almost hanged up. "Are you drunk?"

"Sorry, I thought you were…" she muttered, "how are you? Are you in Kampala now?"

"Yes, I am"

"Free boy!" She teased in a deep voice that sounded like she just woke up.

"How's Solo?" I demanded ignoring her comment.

"Solo is fine. He is sleeping. He's finally starting school in January," she answered in a pleasant tone.

"Cool. Shola, when will this war between you and daddy end?" I tried to sound much older.

"Look who's talking. At least I know I am at war. Boy, you need help," Shola poked in a condescending manner. I noticed she was intentionally trying to invoke my temper.

"What are you talking about?"

"I thought you hate being called 'boy'. How come you are not quarrelling?" She teased.

"What does that have to do with this? Anyway, I just felt it is unfair to Solo not to know his grandfather"

"You've really grown up, big boy, but I think you should mind your own business," she remarked coldly.

"Ok, I better get going."

"That's quick."

"Yap."

"Ok. Bye. Use a condom!" She concluded laughing like a drunk.

I hung up.

My father called Shola a cheap slut who only went to school to fool around with hopeless boys destined to die from drug overdoses, STDs or a bullet before they made twenty. She got pregnant in her final year of high school; she said it happened when her boyfriend then was consoling her after she told him about our parents' illness. She wanted to forget everything; the fact that they might die soon, my mother's innocence and her inability to do anything for them. Her boyfriend, Robert got her drunk and had his way she, claimed. She told my parents a few weeks later and my father exploded and she exploded in return. She told him she inherited her loose morals from him. She left home and stayed with Robert whose parents lived in the United States of America. After high school before the baby was born, he went to America and she was meant to join him but was denied a visa. From then, she turned as coarse as sand in jogging shoes. Robert got another girl in America and they got engaged about a year ago. According to Shola, the new girl looks like a pole dancer. How she knows, I will never know. She hates men with a passion, starting with our father. She goes through boyfriends like a love novel, one at a time, sometimes two. Some beat her up. Some just walk away never to return. Someone always comes back to give my mother the 'scoop'.

Every time my mother thinks of Shola, she shatters into tears. I always wished she was the same person in the playhouse, but she is not, she doesn't have a trace of the Shola that saved me from Pete's slaps and kicks. I remember once when I was in the third grade and Shola was in the eighth, she gave me her raincoat on our way back home while she got soaked in the rain. Back then I felt it was her job to protect me, but now it felt like I should have been the one to look out for her. Her ways of dealing with issues are always to implode and then finally explode when she's had it. The explosion can be triggered by just calling her names. She wanted to do Industrial Art and Design in college and always made Christmas cards for everybody she knew including me. The last Christmas card I received from her was five years ago. I now send her cards every Christmas, Valentine and birthdays with no reciprocation. It's awkward when we meet. I can't find the words to speak, mother just cries and Shola pokes at me making fun of everything from my shoes to my name. Sometimes she sounds so immature, a far cry from who she was. When she is talking to mother, she calls father 'your husband' and always seems to brush aside any attempt to get her to make peace with him. Shola was our father's pride and joy. An assertive, yet calm and reserved disposition that exuded self-importance. She also borrows from my mother's strength which in most cases can be considered their weaknesses. She has the ability to stick to what she truly believes and will not waver for a second. Like my father, she never shows any sign of feeling hurt or even crying, at least not in a while. I always wondered if she cried at night when she was in bed with Solo, alone, feeling like the whole world was congested with traitors who just want to hurt people. I just don't know how to help her, but I have to do something. She's too young to be alone and hating already.

***

Helen came over and she sat with us in the sitting room for about two hours watching rap videos on Channel O, and Channel 5, which we alternated. She smelled like something that came out of a sweet factory. It seemed like a concoction of strawberries and flowers. Boko wanted to watch TBN and I wanted to watch Mnet, but Kintu kept on saying 'five more minutes'. It sounded too noisy, but Helen and Kintu where completely enchanted by the songs. Boko and I left them indoors after accepting the fact that their five minutes might be five hours. Kintu said we would be going 'clubbing'. He said he had 'proggie' in the next hour and we were planning to leave Boko at home with the TV. Kintu did not want to involve him in ungodly matters. What he did not want to say out loud was that Boko's mere presence would dampen the nightclub and make the night out feel like a visit to the dentist without anesthesia.

Boko and I sat outside on the balcony overlooking Madam Shuweta's little garden trying to admire the night sky. I was hoping he would not mention the day he found me crying in the school cafeteria. I always hoped he didn't and had never, so far. In the arid night, kind winds blew like a compassionate stranger offering a cool drink of water in return for nothing. The least I could do was to smile at such kindness and re-adjust myself to embrace it all. The wind provided a magnificently cool embrace; with nothing in return but the willingness to sit and spend the time. For a moment I felt like I was being scrubbed clean by its waves upon waves. I only realized how silly my smiling seemed when I saw Boko through my peripheral vision stealing glances at me and probably wondering what was so interesting.

"Is TBN, Turner Broadcasting Network?" I asked attempting to start a conversation.

"No, It's Trinity Broadcasting Network," Boko replied with his eyes fixed on the sky.

"Oh, yes my mother watches it too, it's a good channel!" I tried to appease him. Boko looked at me, smiled and then returned to the sky.

The stars reminded me of the sky in Koto's village. He said they were like a black mourning dress with diamond tears sprinkled over it, mourning the passing away of wisdom. Koto told me every human had a star in the heavens and that the stars were the spirits of each person.

As we caught a glimpse of a shooting star sizzling across the sky, I told Boko that a shooting star was a falling star and meant someone somewhere had just died. It meant that the star would fall on the person's grave and be buried with that person. I also told him about how the bright stars belonged to important, rich and famous people and how the dull stars belonged to an unknown like him and I. The expression on his face showed that he really did not agree with the mythical tale, but he smiled as though he admired its creativity. I didn't believe the story either, but Koto believed it with his entire being, though he had never been to his own village before. He always said he wished all the stars that belonged to his villagers would fall out of the sky in a day, because of what they did to great-grandmother.

"What happens after the star is buried with the person?" Boko asked as if he was curious.

"They wake up in the after."

"Afterlife?"

"Yes, the Grand Fields of the Ancestors!" I told him with a dramatic expression on my face to show him how awesome it was.

"Really! And what do they do in the Grand Fields? Have you been there?"

"No! Of course not. They know all mysteries and see all things"

"…And then?" he asked as if he wanted me to continue with the list.

"I think that's all. I don't really know. My gardener told me that." I tried to save face.

"So, where will you go when you die?" He asked me and that made me very nervous.

"Are you trying to scare me? Well, I don't know!" I stated, "Maybe heaven! Where will you go?" I asked him.

"Definitely heaven!" He whispered as if he was just recalling a lover's promise and gave a natural smile.

"What makes you so sure?"

"Because I believe in Jesus, the Son of God who died for my sins," he sounded like one of the TBN programs and reminded me of the suede suit preacher.

"But what makes you so sure!"

"Well, I know that I know that I know!"

"I wished I had your assurance!" I declared as I recalled my mother once told me the same thing. She said she knew heaven was waiting for her and went on about the beautiful things she believed were there. At times I think she could be suicidal, but she is not. She is only embracing her fate. I think.

The smell of pork, and chips, mixed with beer and cigarettes began blowing in the wind and the dry smoky smell of the burnt oil and fat gave me a mild stomach upset. I could hear the tipsy celebration of the people in the corner bars and their discussion on politics. They were arguing about the local elections, a second term in the constitution and the significance of the African Union. The magnitude of their drunkenness was revealed by the enormity of their lies, as they constantly barked at each other in their selfish attempts to project an image of intellectual enlightenment.

"You know, if we Africans ever work as one, in five years this continent will be as developed as those European countries," a sluggish voice announced.

"No! According to the NDISF statistics of 1999, it will take just one year and six months with the beneficial natural resources we have, the eradication of corruption on the grass root level and hard work in…" the second voice objected.

"That's a lie! It will take seven months and a few days with good communications and the implementation of the 7/7 protocol…it happened in that country in eastern Europe…their President was a certain Chairman Mao who was a relentless man of vision. He…." The third voice interrupted.

"Which eastern European country was that?" Another drinker enquired in curious hostility.

"I don't remember the name, but it was in the Middle East or Europe," he hesitated.

"The reason you don't remember is because no such country ever existed! What will a Chinese head of state be doing leading a European or Middle Eastern nation, or whichever nation you called it?" A voice yelled. The crowd swept in laughter, hands slamming on the tables.

"You must be very foolish to doubt my knowledge, you son of a village peasant. I have read more books than your entire family will ever manage to read in two lifetimes!" He yelled in an uproar, "I would have shown you who I am today, but I am just here to mingle with you commoners and I would not want an uneducated fool like you to waste your pocket change of a salary in the hospital."

“Be easy Chief. Forgive and forget,” a voice soaked in local brew slurred out.

"By the way, what's the 7/7 protocol and NDISF?" An inebriated female voice called out with a chuckle.

"Who are you, Mr. Educated?" A hostile voice demanded, ignoring the female voice and reigniting the argument.

"Come down, honourable, there has to be at least one person to object to a view, that is democracy. We need it in Africa to heal the very marrows of our political system," a rough textured voice tried to mediate.

“Gentlemen, drink up before the beer settles down”, the female voice of a bar attendant falsely advised in the hope of refilling their cups.

The arguments went on, with laughs, coughs and angry outbursts from politics and sex to marriage and war.

***

The flux shimmering orchestration of creaking crickets, croaking frogs, screeching glasses on ceramic tables and drunk men arguing was a fairly restless atmosphere. Their conversations were woven together in Luganda, English and Swahili. The smell of assortments of roast meat and cigarettes probably reminded Boko about my smoking, so he asked me if I really smoked, and I had to confess to him. He said he knew since he had not seen or smelt any cigarette since we arrived.

Boko's parents at first disproved his faith because they were Muslims. He said he used to feel so empty before and that the day he met God, he realized that he had been missing so much in his life. He said Jesus and God were there, no matter what. Even when he thought he was all alone that Jesus, the Holy Spirit, God and his angel were all there to back him up. I was a little scared, and I looked around to make sure they were not as visible as he made it sound.

“How do you know?” I had to inquire.

“Well, God is everywhere and he made everything.”

“So? How is that possible?” I am a Christian but I still had to ask, since it all sounded new to me. They never mentioned that in the Easter shows and Christmas services I attended. Boko told me that everything a human does in his or her life is God-ordained way before the person was born. God knew that we were coming to Uganda and he knows what will happen. It sounded like fiction to me. I was almost certain he watched the suede preacher's sermon.

"What's the point of trying if everything is pre-destined?" I questioned to a deaf ear.

"Have you ever been in a situation and everything seems to point to one direction or person?"

"Well. Yes…"

"That is most likely God trying to tell you something. He is trying to tell us something every second of the day."

"You mean God speaks to people?"

"Yes!"

"Isn't that for people like Moses, and the Bible people?"

"No not only them. It's for every human to communicate with God, but we never pay attention, then when things go wrong, we blame God", he tried to justify.

"What accent does he use?" I asked teasingly. Boko rolled his eyes out of irritation.

I had to change the topic; it seemed as if he was about to start preaching to me, and that was the last thing I wanted to hear. God's plan has had its share in my life; I don't need any more self-righteous burdens dangling on my conscience.

I tried to draw his attention to a drunkard urinating on our neighbour's garden downstairs. We laughed. Then Boko told me that God loves the drunk man and that God has done everything to make the man come into communion with Him, just as he is trying to with me and everybody on earth. *Whatever.*

"If God loves people that much why do bad things happen to innocent people of all people! Why do people die of sickness, famine, wars and all the other natural disaster?" I asked trying to reduce the tremor in my voice.

"We are all sinners and guilty, do you mean you have never ever done or thought of anything bad before? And people's disobedience to God causes most of the problems. If you jump down from a building, what do you expect will happen? The same applies to God. There are always consequences for our actions." He tried to teach me.

"Yeah, typical!"

"What's typical?"

"God's plan, his love, his mercy, grace, forgiveness, BUT

you still have to face consequences for your actions. So, what is the point of forgiveness?" I almost yelled at him.

He said that was why God in his mercy, sent his only son, Jesus to die for the sins of the world. And that on the cross where Jesus was nailed, that all my sins, sicknesses, failures and wrongs, and that of everybody else were atoned for. All we had to do was have faith by believing he did it for us. God did all this because he loved us and that he does not want the devil to have a hold on anyone, he said, because it was through our sins, disobedience to God and the failure to believe that God exists that made us prey to the devil and hell.

"The devil will do anything to make you believe he and God do not exist and if you believe God exists, he will make you blame God for anything that goes wrong in your life. Have you ever heard of anyone blaming the devil for the mishaps? No! They only blame God, though the devil or their own actions caused it," Boko explained.

"Tola, if there is any time in history to believe in God, it is now. There are so many temptations, sicknesses, civil unrest, unforgiveness and the list goes on and all we have to do is accept Gods offer of salvation," he declared as though he was speaking to a congregation.

All I had to do was accept it, believing Jesus did it all on my behalf. And relax. The burdens would go. Jesus would lift them for me. For me?

The conversation came to a halt when our neighbour from downstairs proclaimed a deafening cry at the drunk man easing himself in her garden. She stoned him; the man grumbled some words at her and staggered off holding his head. We laughed. She saw us and restrained her anger.

Kintu told us she was the type of wife who played the man of the house. She was artificial, apart from her excessive makeup. She had a hollow smile that made her look retarded. Kintu said she was always nagging her husband whenever he came home drunk or late, and he normally passed out on the kitchen floor. She would come knocking at our flat at odd hours dressed in lingerie to ask for sugar or salt.

She would go on about being bored since there was nothing to do, so she decided to cook something and then she realized there was no salt or sugar for the tea. Whenever he gave her the sugar or the salt, she always asked, *do you want to come for tea?* His answer had always been, *no, thank you ma'am,* but she had never shown any sign of relenting. She hated it when she was called *Madam*. She said it made her feel too old, so he should call her, *Shuweta*. He called her *Madam Shuweta* instead. I was surprised Kintu would ever pass over an offer to have 'tea' with a woman at such hours, and I still didn't believe he turned her down unless she never asked him. He possibly fabricated the whole story. Back in Kenya, Kintu always talked about girls, how they loved him, and how many he had been with. A lot of students consulted him for tips on getting a girl. I consulted him when Christie broke up with me, and he told me to drink and be 'merry', to let her know I was having a wonderful time now that I was vacant. She would get jealous and come back. She never did.

***

Madam Shuweta seemed to believe she had an ageless beauty, but I guess she had just been avoiding the truth. Kintu said he would give her what she really wanted one of these days, whatever that was, and not sugar or salt.

"Hello guys", Madam Shuweta called out, trying to suppress her Indian accent, after finding her way up the stairs successfully, trying to catch her breath. Boko and I replied in unison, which made us sound like primary school boys, about to receive a lesson from a teacher, "Good evening, Madam Shuweta!"

"A lovely evening it is. I was just coming to ask for sugar from Kintu when I saw that silly man pissing in my garden." She tried to explain the stoning incident, "I hope you boys don't think I am bothering you too much about sugar, it's just that I cannot do without some tea before going to bed. It keeps me warm at night, especially since these nights are becoming very cold." She sounded erotic and I tried not to recall the porn movies we used to watch at sleepovers back in high school. Boko and I had to smile although I did not feel like it and nodded as if we really understood what she was saying.

"Let me get the sugar," and Boko ran in to get the sugar while she stared at me with her retarded smile without blinking her eyes. Her eyeballs were drawn out with dark mascara and her eyelashes were longer than average. It made me shy and I looked down at my feet.

"You sound Nigerian! Are you Nigerian, yeah?" She asked as if we were just meeting for the first time. Boko introduced her to us the very moment we arrived in the building. I told her who I was, but that I had lived in Kenya most of my life, for the second time.

"Nigerians are very clever and great lovers too, that is if they are not the criminal type," she said. I laughed, but she wasn't joking and I had to clear the smile away from my face into my mind. What an awkward lady! That was news to me and I still question why that was the first thing that came to her mind about Nigerians! I was expecting her to talk about the conmen, drugs, witchcraft and other Nigerian stereotypes. Great lovers, she said!

"I used to have a Nigerian boyfriend when I was in college in Belgium. He was very romantic, athletic and intelligent, that was before my family moved to Congo where I met my husband." I didn't know how to answer or what comment to make. I said, "ok"

"Are you like that too? Like the other Nigerians?"

"I don't know," I replied shyly as I wished Boko would return sooner.

"Well, I think it is the food, is it fufu, yeah? Or what is it called?"

"Yes, fufu, but I doubt if it's what made your boyfriend strong", I was about to recommend the possibility of steroids or viagra, when Boko returned with the sugar in a plastic container. I felt relieved since I did not know where the conversation would lead.

"His name was Daré, do you know any Nigerian by that name?" She asked as if she was really expecting me to know.

"Who's he?" I asked as I cleared my thought.

"My ex-boyfriend!" She smiled at full volume.

"Actually, there are a lot of Dares in Nigeria and around the world that are Nigerians." I tried to dissolve the conversation, ignoring my maternal uncle is called Dare too. She would probably say it could be him, which I doubted as he had never been out of Nigeria. He was not the type to write his phone number on a hundred-dollar bill as she claimed her boyfriend did. He was the quiet type. Uncle Dare was the sort that showed up at parties for the food and nothing else. He threw around pleasantries like 'you have lost weight' on weddings to the female relatives and told the men how much more muscular they looked, even when the obvious potbellies were peeping through unbuttoned shirts. At funerals, he told everyone how gracious they looked and then attributed it to the 'glory of God' on them. In all his pleasantries, his direction was always towards the food table and his preference was to be left alone once he arrived there. He always gave me a condescending look, as though I was in the wrong place. He studied the room from a vantage point next to the jollof rice and beverages. When I chatted with him, he always gave me a forced smile and told me to 'run along' halfway through the lackluster conversation.

"Well, I hope we will get to know each other better, yeah! And don't be shy to come and visit", she said with a fixed retarded smile on her face. She gave Boko a quick thanks, by patting his hand and as slowly as she could, she walked down the stairs to her flat holding the plastic container as though it was a delicacy.

Boko told me that Kintu and Helen were no longer watching T.V. I wasn't interested, but Boko tried to reason that Lydia's friend could be in the toilet and maybe Kintu went to pick up something in his room. That made me realize what he was implying.

***

We checked the sitting room and the toilet but there was no trace of Helen or Kintu. We tried to listen at Kintu's door and we heard the faint squeaking of Kintu's spring mattress on his metal bed while Jay-Z was playing in the background. Boko was upset and he said he was leaving the flat as soon as he found another place because he could not tolerate such immoral behaviour. He wanted to go in and stop them, but I told him to just calm down and we would speak to Kintu later or in the morning. I thought Boko needed to loosen up.

I woke up feeling so empty, maybe it was because I missed home, or it could be the fact that Kintu's mother reminded me of my mother in some ways. She was as caring as my mother was and she encouraged us to look out for each other. I lay on the bed staring at the ceiling; it was white with interlockings and a light bulb pointing down like a pendulum.

Then I felt occupied.

The black and white painting of an old wooden cabin by a lake that was hanging on the wall looked perfect, in the sense that it looked very real. I seemed to have just noticed it for the very first time since my mother bought it for me. She said she bought it for me because she knew I loved the playhouse and the painting looked like it, she thought it would be the perfect present for me. I liked it because it was art, not because it looked like the playhouse. I now realize that the lines, shades, dots, and curves that made up the house in the painting were truly remarkable. I actually felt like an art critic. It all made perfect sense.

"The shades of grey are the artistic expression of his secret grieving and the white patches are the places of sincerity he has found in his life- his work. I would say the poetic scenery captures the artist's life. The lake, his tears; the wretched cabin, his situation; the cloudy skies, his hopelessness. I would say the artist knows other things, unlike…Mr Kintu the sex addict", it tried to imitate a British art professor's accent. My silly tone and gestures made me laugh at myself. I felt a bit crazy laughing alone.

I could hear Boko singing hymns in the shower with the talent of an angelic choir boy yet to meet puberty and Kintu asking him to keep it down or save it for Church. It warmed my heart and I smiled when I realized it was almost a playhouse in itself since my sister and I were always bothered by each other's pleasures. Tea parties and construction sites don't get along well. One had to give way to the other.

It reminded me of my family and I felt like seeing them all at once and telling them I love them, but I was not sure if I really did. There was something missing that I couldn't really put my finger on. We are all messed up, thanks to my father.

I was frightened by the thought of what happened yesterday, Madam Shuweta and then Kintu and Helen, there seems to be more in this playhouse than childish remarks and quarrels. Maybe this is the 'Workhouse', after all Kintu is burning a lot of energy, so he is working, I chuckled at my thought. I finally found it impossible to believe that Kintu actually turned down Madam Shuweta's offer of having tea. He couldn't even keep his hands off Lydia's friend. He'd go for anything in a dress. Just like my father. I always suspected from the way Mrs Njoroge always hovered around him, overdressed and soaked in perfume. The way my mother would sigh when he grabbed his car keys from the wooden bowl on the coffee table to 'finish up at work' on Sunday afternoon or Saturday night. I noticed he never made eye contact with anyone of us. He normally had a blank look on his face, like he was a drone on autopilot.

The bell rang. Since Boko was in the shower and Kintu was occupied with Helen, I got it. I tried to listen in to the ringing bell by Kintu's door on my way, but it was silent. I had a feeling it was probably Madam Shuweta wanting salt for her morning eggs or wanting to invite us to something.

I was stunned when I opened the door and it was Lydia. I had to scream out loud, "Lydia! How are you?" Hoping that Kintu would hear. Lydia seemed surprised. She ignored my fake salutation and asked for Kintu; she did not wait for my response. She dragged past me in an eloquent manner that for a moment I thought she was royalty. Her posture was upright and chin rested on the horizon that it pointed to. I felt like a lowly doorman and a bad one at that. I should have announced her arrival and ushered her in with a gracious wave of the hand, just before I gave her bow.

I followed closely to see what would become of Kintu. Lydia had an aggravated look on her face and I knew she had suspected something. We bumped into Boko in the passage peeping neck first from the toilet door, Lydia seemed to get more suspicious and she walked faster to the end of the passage and burst into Kintu's room without knocking.

She shut the door firmly behind her. Boko and I waited for a scream, clash or exchange of words; anything to show that Kintu was receiving the thrashing of his life. Amazingly enough there was nothing. Boko and I stared at each other; we were most likely thinking the same thing; how odd they all are in Kintu's room. Boko went back into the bathroom looking even more displeased with the incident and nodding his head aggressively in disapproval. I thought his head would fall off.

"I am going to tell his mother!" He muttered and slammed the door.

After waiting a while longer at Kintu's door, I peeped into the keyhole just to see with my own eyes what the three of them were doing in the same room. I could only see Kintu's feet at the edge of his bed and Lydia's shoes and what looked like her handbag on the floor. How unroyal; to leave the royal handbag on the floor! I could not see the third person, so I just assumed she was also on the bed doing some strange things, in the closet or lying about something since Kintu is a very good liar. He might have cooked up some story, but whatever that tale was, I had to give it to him, it must have been a very good one.

I speculated what happened to the fear of AIDS or pregnancy these days like an old miserable and perhaps a grumpy man with a hint of repulsive envy. "I hope he bought more condoms," I thought to myself. He showed off empty boxes of condoms to Boko and I. He said he was out of supplies; he kept the empty boxes as trophies, to show 'how much love he was getting'. 'Crazy boy,' I heard myself whisper and could almost see myself wondering what to do next like a decrepit old man dazed by the traffic.

I decided to return to my room and finish up my morning stretching on the bed. I took one last peep through the keyhole; I could see nothing. Boko was back to his church hymns, and it seemed to actually irritate me too. How could anyone sing church hymns when someone in the same house was getting laid! I felt a righteous repulse towards all the people in the house. I am the only sane one.

My heart found its way to my throat when I found Helen in my room; she had only her underwear on. She gave me a forced shy smile; though she wasn't. I felt like killing Kintu, and at the same time, I felt the urge to use one of the movie lines to break the ice. After swallowing heavily with the help of a gallon of saliva, my heart was almost flipping sides under my ribcage, but it was better there than in my throat.

I tried to show her I was not interested and definitely not scared. I asked her why she wasn't dressed. She told me her clothes were still in Kintu's closet, with her arms crossing her breast. When I saw her cleavage, my heart seemed to stop for a moment and then suddenly started beating, but very fast erratically. Wild fantasies came to my head; I tried my best to think of the picture on the wall, it wasn't as important anymore.

I offered her my T-shirt to wear. I felt the blood rolling through my veins as I tried very hard to clear my mind of the wrong pictures going through my head. I tried again to stare at the charcoal drawing on the wall, but it seemed like scribbles of black and grey on a white paper in a frame.

"Can I lie down on your bed?" She asked when I finally sat down on the bed to reduce the weight on my nervous legs. I said 'yes', and sprang up from the bed and sat on the floor. She laughed softly. I got more nervous. She asked why I was sitting on the floor, that she doesn't bite. I recalled Nzeli threatening me at Steers over the french-fries and fried chicken I bought her. Helen asked if I was afraid. Not as much as I was of Nzeli. I told her I was not. I returned to the bed and laid down at the very edge since it was a single and I did not want to get too close. I wanted to show her I was not afraid. I felt cold and my stomach seemed to be in pandemonium. I felt I needed the toilet badly.

"Won't you fall?" She asked as she turned her whole body to face me. I would have gone for my bath, but that would require me to undress and she could say she wanted to join me and end up undressing in front of me. If I went to Boko's room, he would most likely go on about how God is not pleased with the activities taking place in the flat. Going to the living-room would be a bad idea since she would most likely follow me and Boko would end up thinking I had sex with her. Well, I didn't really mind what he thought, but I didn't feel like going to the living room.

She stretched her honey brown hand and pulled me closer. It was warm. I could hear my heart beating and I was trying everything to stop my hands from trembling. She smiled. I was sweating and at the same time cold.

“Do you have a girlfriend?” She asked as if it really mattered.

“No! I mean yes! Christie, her name is Christie.”

"It seems you don't really like her since you are doubting."

"I love her and I think of her all the time." I tried to cover up, though I felt like telling her the truth. Christie had no clue I still existed and she would probably not remember who I was if I tried initiating conversation with her. I remember Christie and I agreeing not to have sex before marriage. She came up with the idea and I agreed for no reason. I always lied to the guys at school that I had gone ‘all the way' several times with her. There was always a round of high-fives and others shared their exploits, a lot of which seemed fictional. I remember Daniel Barlow, a classmate in the 10th grade who said an air hostess offered him ‘membership' to the ‘mile-high club'. All the boys in the changing room went crazy and everyone wanted a step-by-step account. I had no clue what the mile-high club was but like all the other boys, I wanted Daniel to be my best friend. He became the life of every party and was often asked to share that mile-high club experience at every opportune moment. Girls liked following each other to the powder room, boys followed the guy who had the mile-high club experience everywhere! There is one thing I know about teenage boys since that time, they are always curious about sex and would lie to their friends to make it look like they know everything about it. The guy who knows the most, or claims to, becomes the coolest and probably heads the clique by virtue of his experience, be it truth or fiction. I led the clique at one point, knowing full well that I had never as much as kissed a girl, not to mention sex. But the boys followed my lead in ignorant bliss, taking advice from me that I had and would have never taken myself.

"How come I don't see any of her pictures in your room?" She demanded with a soft wink at me after staring at the drawing on the wall. I guess she knew I was lying and she knew I could not resist my urge. Her brown complexion looked radiantly appealing. She moved closer, slowly, and closer. I closed my eyes. I pretended to be asleep or dead. The most recent picture of Christie I had was taken in the ninth grade. If I showed her, she'd think I was a pedophile. Christie and I took the picture the day she broke up with me; she wore a forest green fleece jacket over her green t-shirt and Gucci marble jeans. I wished I had apologized right away, but no, I felt my immature accusations were grounded in facts, but it was just one of Koto's idle talks I took too seriously. She walked away red in the face into the toilet and that was the end. The end of us.

***

Koto used to tell me that women have a certain mystical power over men and that once they start to seduce you, you are nothing but a slave. They make you feel like you are the one in control, but really, they are the puppet masters and because the man gets applauded on stage, he feels he has done it all by himself. The real applaud goes to the puppet master. I never understood him then; I just looked at girls with a certain irritation because of their snobbish ways and their annoying giggles. I initially asked Christie to 'be my girl', only because all the guys in the movies had girls. It was only after we broke up that I realized I loved her. Whatever that meant.

Koto said he knew that Mrs. Njoroge could be HIV positive and the rumours were all over town that her husband had died of AIDS and not cancer as she claimed. Still, there was that string that turned into a cord, which pulled him towards her. The silly coy voice saying it was meant to be every time she offered him a drink. The fact that she deliberately dropped signs that she fancied him. He said he tried everything to ignore her existence, he avoided her, but she always came looking for him and invited him to help do some things in her garden. Sometimes, he said he felt as if he would let anything happen between them, just for a few minutes. Sometimes, he got scared of the price he would have to pay for his raging lust for a forbidden thing, but her scent, smile and her appearance made him feel she possibly wasn't sick. No way she could have AIDS. He said she was the prettiest woman he had seen and her mere presence made him want to tell her how pretty she was. A high-class woman wanting him and making passes was almost a dream. It could mean he would never have to break his back digging gardens anymore. He said it was easier to justify the wrong things when there were benefits at stake. He was a prisoner to his own desires, they controlled him, they answered the questions and they found the solutions even if they were temporary and carried mist in their substance. Back then the logic must have been solid like a diamond, though cloudy.

I remember him staggering across the backyard with his shirt blood red. I asked him what happened; he said he was going to die. He told me I was too young to understand, but the verdict had been drawn concerning his life, he was as good as dead. The HIV result flapped in his back pocket like an unwanted pay cheque, cursed by its issuer. He probably wished his name was not on it and it had nothing to do with him. But it did. The test confirmed what he knew but ignored and then eventually denied. Now the truth stared him in the eyes like the barrel of a loaded gun that had already been fired, the question was when the bullet would hit its target.

"My family has been cursed ever since my great grand mama's days, there is nothing I can do to prevent it", he kept on telling me.

"Prevent what?" I asked almost crying, troubled by his anguish.

"I was bewitched. I have AIDS," he yelled, his voice like drought. His words crumbled like dust and the particles pulled tears from my eyes.

That was the first time I had ever seen him crying. He looked as if he had been forced to do something he would have never dared to do. His crying hummed like a deep vibration across the backyard that day as he punched away at my playhouse and I just stood there not knowing what to do. My soaked face was consoled by the palms of my hands. His punches made holes that looked like little circular windows that the sunrays stretched through. It was like he told me, 'More windows will appear as you grow older in the playhouse,' but he made them.

I thought he was going crazy, but he was only drunk; an attempt to bury his grief and summon courage which surely failed. That day my parents got worried and thought he was out of his mind too; they told him to take a few days off and go and stay elsewhere. Poor Koto had nowhere else to go than to the same woman who had sealed his fate. He probably scratched his ear when he got drunk, since he had the tendency to go drinking on his salary and overreacting when he was drunk. That day was extreme, Koto was never hostile or aggressive; he only disagreed and argued with anyone about anything when he was drunk. He punched holes in my playhouse, I almost hated him, but I could not, he helped build it, I thought in my young mind. He was my friend.

That was the last time he told me anything about his village because that was the last time I was allowed to see him. My parents, especially my father saw to it that I did not interact with him. He said Koto was a loose cannon, that he was not a good example, and that he was a threat to our family.

***

I don't have a condom. What if she gets pregnant? What if Helen is HIV positive? I didn't want to end up like Koto. What if something happened, anything, I wondered in the silence of my mind and I could hear my thoughts echoing at the back of my head like an empty shell. Still, I wanted to let go and see what sex was really like; at least I would have something to tell my grandchildren and I wouldn't change the conversation next time Kintu talked about sex.

She kissed me. I trembled and she held me with her warm hands to stay still. I could taste nicotine in her kiss and her tongue swam in my mouth like an electric eel, searching for my soul. I was afraid it would find my heart roaming like a schizophrenic in my throat. My heart so quick to forget that it longed for Christie. Helen dragged herself and lay on me and I felt all her body on me. Everything became blank in my head and the echoes died down, all I saw was black, and all I heard was silence. I was dead. Her hand began to move down between my legs. At that moment, it seemed I did not care anymore; I just wanted to do it. Whatever it was. I felt like I was drowning in warm water, it felt so nice, but I felt mild burning itches at the back of my chest or somewhere. I felt like I was in one of those dreams. It felt like something was not right. It felt like when I was a child and was not sure if I was peeing in my dream or it was really on my bed. She dipped her hands into my boxer. I wanted to say 'No', but all I felt and heard was 'Yes.' I wondered where God and those angels Boko told me about where?

I wondered where God was when Koto's family was cursed for doing nothing wrong. Where was he when Shola was denied a visa, where was he when Robert got her pregnant. I wondered where he was when my mother prayed, when I killed the innocent bird.

I wondered where God was when my father was busy messing around with Mrs. Njoroge. I wondered where God is when a human dies after living a life devoted to God; when a human is killed because of honesty, truth, faithfulness and sincerity to God. Nobody is perfect! I wondered where God was right now. The words echoed in my head again, as if I was hollow and I could feel the echo vibrating as I thought of God. *Where is God right now?*

I was crying. I don't know why. Helen looked puzzled and even shocked and her hand stood limply in mid-air. Through the blub of tears, I could see her mouth opened in bemusement. I thought I heard her say "sorry" faintly as she began to retrieve her seduction. She must have felt she wasted it on me, a crybaby. I don't think she ever met a guy who cried like I did before. She looked at me with a scared pitiful eye that said I must be sick in the mind. The same look a scared woman would give a violently crazy man approaching her from across the pavement. Jumping into the coming traffic would be a better option she probably thought.

There was a knock on the door.

I was scared.

I thought it was God knocking.

"Tola, are you there? Are you still going with me to church?"

It was Boko. Never in my life had I ever appreciated hearing his voice, but still, there was something in me that made me angry, he interrupted. Helen rolled off me swiftly and I fell on the floor. That was confirmed by a mild thump.

Boko opened the door when he heard her body thump on the floor. I thought he was shocked at the sight and the fact that Helen was in my room, on the floor with my t-shirt on. I guess he was most likely wondering where the world was going- to hell. He paused and stared at Helen, muttered a greeting or an insult, I was not sure. She smiled as she stood up and lay on the bed with her face down as if she wanted him out of the room. I realized how short my t-shirt was when her underwear caught my attention.

"Tola, can I talk to you for a minute?" Boko's voice ordered like a drill sergeant.

"Ok," I replied as I stood up from the bed trying not to touch Helen in any way and hoping not to flare Boko's imagination. I felt like a puppet being directed with strings.

I felt like I was empty and there was nothing else left for me to do. I felt tired. I was fed up. I was blank. I was just doing anything for the sake of anything. I considered the possibility of me having been cursed. Just like Koto, but for what? Who on earth have I wronged?

No wonder he said that when I left the playhouse, I would see things in a clearer light. I would come to the realization of the things I had been ignorant of. They said she had cancer, just like Mr. Njoroge did. Koto found out what that meant. I guess now I see why my father could not even stand in the same room with my mother every time he returned from his drinking club. That must have been why he never looked into my eyes when he talked to me and he spent most of his time at the Social Drinkers Club because he felt guilty. No wonder my mother was worried I was leaving home because she was afraid. Guilty, because he cheated on her, and afraid because she thought she would lose me like she lost my father. Now I see. Somehow.

There used to be a time when my father could stand in the same room with my mother and stare into her eyes and tell her how much he loved her without saying a word. His eyes would light up her face and she would smile at him, but he would just stare at her in a trance as if he had just seen her for the first time. If my mother was white, I guess she would have all the blood in her body flushed into her face. She would have to tell him to stop it before he would ever think of stopping. Was he acting it all out?

"Stop looking at me like that, you are making me laugh?" She would chuckle like a schoolgirl, trying to hide her smile.

"It's not my fault God made you this beautiful!" He would argue.

Was he already cheating on her then? Did he act all that out or was his story true about it being the first time he ever did such a thing?

"Okay, thank you, but stop!"

"I don't know how to", he would try to explain. My sister, Shola and I would laugh and say, 'daddy is in love,' through our missing teeth.

"See, even the children are laughing at you. Stop looking like that!" she would say, trying her very best to stop herself from laughing by putting up a serious front.

"Let them laugh at me, they will understand why I am the luckiest man one day," he would say with his hands wide open as if he was acting one of those Bollywood musicals.

"I think mommy is in love too because she is shy", Shola would say trying to cover her missing milk-teeth while laughing.

"It is not my fault your daddy is that handsome either", she would tease too.

"I will marry a handsome man like daddy too," Shola would say in her innocence. Maybe the handsome ones were the problem; she must have pondered when she grew older. They are like keeping sugar in your pocket; ants are bound to come; or maybe it's their fathers. She once asked me if I was like our father. I did not know what she meant at first till she mentioned Mrs. Njoroge. I told her no, but now I am not sure.

It seemed too long ago, I cannot remember it in colour anymore, and everything looks just like the black and white drawing. It is still beautiful when I think of it, except it seems like a book I read in the past. I recall how my father would stare directly into my eyes and say, 'My son' with all the pride he could summon, which gave me the inspiration to become a man like him one-day. He was transparent then or was I just too young to notice. He was strong, bold with a deep voice that I always tried to imitate. He sounded just like Simba's father in the *Lion King*.

It is as if the colour was drained out of the perfect picture and the black and white left scribbles on white paper; it's a mess. Maybe it's my mind. It's a mess. Beyond a mess!

Shola lives alone because she cannot trust any man. Her third boyfriend was really nice and soft-spoken, but she said he was like that because he cheated. We never knew if he did, since he got tired of not being trusted. The only thing she gained out of the relationship was another pregnancy; she was not sure which of her last three boyfriends it belonged to. Maybe the miscarriage was good news in disguise after all. If it really was a miscarriage! Sometimes I wonder if the problem was really with the men she dates or with her or maybe it's my father's fault that she is finding it hard to trust any man.

And Koto. Where was God when Koto tried his very best to resist the temptation? Maybe he did not ask for help or maybe he had no faith. Where was God when my father was cheating on my mother with Mrs. Njoroge. Where was God when my father sent Koto away because he was jealous that Mrs. Njoroge also had been having an affair with Koto. I wonder who the loose cannon was, him or Koto. Whose fault was all this? All this mess!

I was angry when the thoughts gushed through my mind and a billion words flushed into my echoing head and it became too crowded, I felt like screaming. If my skin wasn't the only one, I had, I would have torn it off without a second thought, but I was afraid of the pain. I felt like my heart was burning. I could even feel the heat sipping through my chest. It would hurt me too much if I ripped it out, but I did not like it there. Burning. Really burning. Or is it a heart attack?

I could not hear Boko clearly; it was as if his voice was going on and off.

"It is not wise to have sex out of marriage," Boko repeated to me, "the consequences can be fatal even if you don't believe in God, and that is why God does not want me, you or anybody else to have sex outside the marriage institution. It's for our own safety"

"Really?" I heard myself. A confused clumsy Nigerian whose life had already been mapped out by his identity, a drug dealer, a conman, visa rejections, cheating father, messed up family. I felt sorry for him, he was I. I felt sorry for myself? I hated the way it sounded. I felt like Judas. Poor Judas, it was his job to betray Jesus. If he didn't, who would? Did he have a choice? He was pre-destined. All his prayers and ambitions could have been to be a better person, but no, destiny or fate came looking for him. And he betrayed Jesus, and he felt miserable and he killed himself. And no one would name their children Judas. I told my mother about the affair: I saw them hugging. Not the type of hug you gave a friend, the types you gave someone you wanted to undress. They looked like two misfits in the rain, almost awkward. Doing the wrong thing at the wrong time with the wrong person in the wrong place. It was all wrong.

"Yes! God cannot force you to do what he wants otherwise he is not God. He will only do it when you ask Him; He will never force His way into your life; He can only warn you and advise you- it's up to you to take it", Boko tried to preach.

His voice continued fading on and off as though I was drifting in and out of a lucid dream.

He told me that as a human I cannot do much on my own because its human nature to sin and it is only when I submit to the will of God that I can start to attain self-control. I thought it was a good excuse to abandon responsibility. He said it is not easy, but if I am willing God is more than willing to help me; God's hands are always wide open to accept me for who I am because He loves me and cares about me. All I had to do was to ask him to come into my heart and into my life; he said God had been knocking at the door of my heart since the day I was born. Was that why my heart was burning? Did he knock on Judas'? Sometimes I feel my heart is glowing amber in the darkness of my body. With every pound, I could almost feel the imaginary pain clutching at my chest. Though it does not hurt, it felt like an engineer being raved and ready to do something outrageous.

I was angry.

"Where was God?" I asked Boko, feeling overwhelmed by tears of confusion and frustration.

"When? Where? Wh... What?" Boko asked confused as he patted me on the back and told me it was ok to cry and that it was better I let out whatever was bothering.

"Where was God? I prayed and prayed, where was He?" I demanded. It was as if all the times my mother took me to church along with her were just a waste of time. I used to pray that God would take care of every one of us and let everything remain perfect. It was me praying for a fist full of water not to drain out. It was hopeless.

"Tola, you can't earn God's favour by going to church. He loves you already, just believe it, that is all he asks," Boko whispered sternly.

"Then why didn't he answer…my prayers."

"I don't know, but I know everything works out for the good of those who love God, just trust him. He is God, he created everything. His wisdom is beyond us, but he tells us he loves us immensely."

"Really?" I sobbed silently and irritated, remembering that Helen, Kintu and Lydia could hear me. I thought Helen may be thinking I was accusing her of rape. Pathetic me! A grown man crying!

"He has always been there! He may not answer when you call, but he is always on time. What the enemy means for evil, God can and will turn it into good." Boko stated sternly, as I remembered my mother made that same statement. Maybe they had been chatting. I hope she did not tell him about her condition. She told the Pastor at her church. When he visited, he asked me how I felt about the whole situation, that it must be affecting me physiologically. I told him I had no idea what he was talking about. He told me God is an ever-present help in trouble. God works silently behind the scenes and his purpose is only revealed at the very end when it all makes sense. I felt like slapping that potty-sized pastor wanna-be on the back of the head. What does he or anyone know about what I feel? It must be 'God's plan' that I slap him on the head. I did not.

I had a dream and I saw myself in dark wooden house with leaking roofs that dripped with dirty water on my head, then I saw a form that looked like that of a man calling me to come out. When I came out of the worn-out house, it was raining, gloomy and there was grey grass as far as my eyes could see. I saw Koto walking towards the horizon where the dark heavy clouds were tackling the earth, shirtless and with a sore-infested back. I was scared and I thought to myself in the dream, *this must be one of those dreams again.* I wanted to wake up. I called Koto, but he was deaf to my voice. He looked and walked like a robot programmed to find where the horizon ends.

A huge sun rose like a massive umbrella from the opposite direction of the cloud Koto was heading to and an entity pointed me to head that direction. Everywhere, the light of the sun flashed on came alive with colour and growth. As I was walked into the light of the sun, I heard my father call.

"Son. Where are you going?"

"None of your business!" I yelled feeling the hair on the back of my neck rise. "Nobody asked you where you were going!" I added. I turned my back to him and walked toward the light, but I noticed sores developing on my hands, going up my arms.

"What is this?" I yelled and my voice echoed like a lost sound in a cave.

"What did I tell you, they were?" the entity replied.

"Who are you?" I asked when I saw clearer, he looked like a reflection on water.

"Who are you!" my question bounced back.

"I am Tola."

"Yes, and that is you," the form pointed to me. Another me, burning and I stood there staring at myself burning. The sores on me erupted and were burning. There was two of me; one with the burning sores and the other closer to the entity.

"Why? Isn't that me?"

"Yes, it is and you're burning with anger and unforgiveness!"

"I am not angry! I am not. Angry at whom?" I yelled in hostility, only realizing after. My voice echoed a long time over and over again. My father's voice called, but I couldn't see him.

"Unforgiveness will kill you. Anger will destroy you." The entity proposed.

"But I am not angry and who have I not forgiven?" I answered petrified.

"Yourself. Your father. Your life."

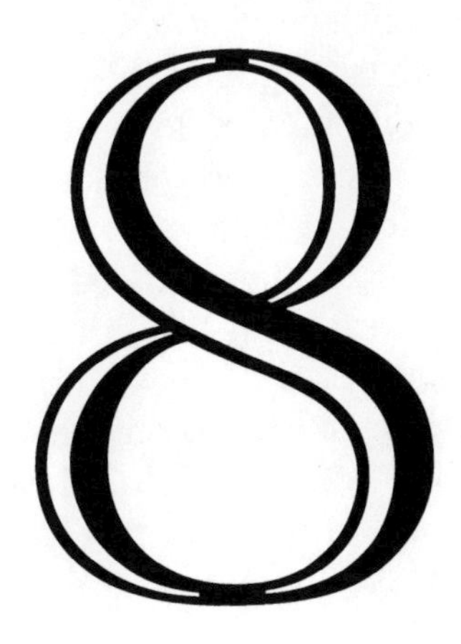

I heard the crying and realized I had fallen asleep in Boko's room while I was weeping, but I wasn't sure if I had been dreaming or else my imagination was playing games on me. It could be the TV I watched. I wasn't sure if I was still dreaming or not. I could still feel the hair on the back of my neck erected when I used my hand. I tucked my hands under the pillow under my head and I could feel a book. I assumed it was a Bible since my mother always placed her Bible under the pillow to enable her to read it before she went to bed. Lying on my back, I stared up at the ceiling and realized there were light brown rings between the white interlocking grids like patterns. According to my knowledge, that meant there was a leak in the roof somewhere and it would only be a while before raindrops started dripping into Boko's room. The dream I just had flashed and I smelled the dampness of the dark wooden house, looking like the cabin in the drawing. Maybe it was, I wasn't certain.

The crying grew louder and I could hear footsteps approaching the door.

"I am dead!"

I got scared. It reminded me of the day Shola and I discovered our parents were HIV positive or at least we thought. It started with my father's footsteps getting louder and louder as he approached the sitting-room; after my mother told Shola and I that they would like to tell us something. Every time a communication came in such a formal tone, we knew something was wrong. Maybe death in the family, terminal illness or the prospect of an unwanted long-term travel. Whatever it was wasn't going to be good. My father had a similar tone on a Friday afternoon when he came to pick me from school. The sad news then was that his aunt, my grand-aunt, the one that coined my nickname of 'imported man' passed away. Though I never heard her use it, every family member claimed she came up with it because I grew up abroad. I only met her thrice. I could, however, remember her indifferent eyes that belittled everything they were cast on, including me, especially me. She never spoke to people, she spoke down to them. She was a puffed up lady who spoke very little and when she spoke she made you feel you were contributing the obvious. This made most people quiet around her. Most of the time she gestured to them like a monarch to bring or give something to someone. Anytime you stared at her, you'd find her eyes were already fixed on you. It always made me cringe!

That formal voice was used again the day my parents delivered the news. My mother was just sobbing on the sofa. My father told us everything; him and Mrs Njoroge, how it started and where it ended. It started after her husband's funeral when he went next door to return some of the things he borrowed from the late. She started crying and he tried consoling her, the next thing they were in the bedroom. It ended when he felt his energy level was not the same and after the annual medical checkup his doctor called and wanted to meet him in person. After the news, I walked out of the house, while Shola was crying out in terror and heaping insults on my father. We both knew people where dying, but I never thought it could happen to anyone in the family. I did not know what to do; I always knew there were a few perfect people. I always thought my dad was one of them. Now I know perfection is a myth and the only faithful man is one that has not been propositioned, myself included. My mother always said Jesus was the only perfect person because Jesus was God. He was perfect, that is why everyone else who believed in him could strive to be perfect by faith in him, but they could never be perfect. They could only get better and better. It sounded like a condition that could never be cured but required resilient hope and gusto. I wondered what the point of trying was. Fighting a fight that could never be won, yet must be fought seemed futile. That evening, I sat outside at the backyard staring at the bird's nest and wishing I had never stabbed the baby bird. I was absolutely convinced that what I did to little *birdie* came back to haunt me. Its slippery body tucked partly in the egg and one of its feet under its wet little fluffy wing and the big dark eyes staring at me. I sat out that day until midnight without knowing it. Shola called me in later and I went to bed without having dinner or saying a word. No words could explain how cracks run and ravage through the heart or how spoken words turn to choking dust in the throat. Why bother trying. Nothing can be said to change the past. Nothing! All I wished was, I had not killed that bird.

It's quite amazing how everybody longs for the past like the smell of lost love or the voice of a soothing soul that can absorb all hurt. Maybe it's because the best times of their lives were in the past. Maybe that was why I was lucky when I was in the playhouse and Koto envied me. Maybe that was why all the older people talk about the moral fabric being destroyed; maybe it's just their way of saying these are the bad times. The bad times are heavy like the dark veil of an omen being hatched. Its fulfilment spewing vilely with intense viscosity into every life clogging everything good and suffocating all hope.

Koto's great-grandmother told his father to always remember, *one never knows how lovely the festival is until the drummers stop and the dance ends.* Koto always said she would tell everyone to dance their very best, eat the most, drink enough and laugh the loudest till they were worn out, to avoid any regrets at the end of it all. Maybe that is what I was supposed to do. Live for the moment. No! Everything is dust!

The door opened.

It was Kintu, followed by Boko. There was much noise and I tried to gain my orientation. All I heard was Boko calling 'Jesus,' and Kintu announcing that he was dead. I could hear Lydia crying in the living room, it almost sounded as if she was giggling with her thin stringed voice.

"I hope you did not have sex with Helen!" Boko yelled as he grabbed me shaking me aggressively. His eyes pointing into mine.

"No! Why...what is…"

"You won't believe it!" Boko interrupted. I nodded that I did not know. And Boko broke the news. Helen was HIV positive. I was astonished and speechless. I did not believe it, because it sounded like a joke or better still a part of the dream. My heart paused and I felt light-headed.

"What?"

"She is HIV positive and Kintu had sex with her, last night. Remember! Without a condom!"

"But how do you know?" I demanded. Since she looked perfectly healthy and she wanted me too.

"Because Lydia thought you were making moves on her, so she told Kintu to advise you that her friend is HIV positive", he continued loudly, "Kintu cried out, 'Hell No!' and Lydia knew what that meant."

"So, you mean Kintu and Lydia too might be infected?" I asked.

"Yes! This is not the first time he did her! I pray God will be merciful," he declared with sweat rolling down his forehead. The married man Helen had an affair with had infected her. He was rich, prominent and had everything a college girl could want. Cars, travels and hotels, he had it all. She wanted to have his baby and took the recommend HIV test; he promised he'd leave his wife if it was a boy. The result was positive, she told him, he faded out and she had an abortion. Her parents never knew.

I felt as remorseful as Kintu, about Helen, Lydia and Shola. I was afraid for Shola because she was no longer the sweet innocent girl that was my sister. I also felt sorry for my parents, Helen's, Lydia's, Kintu's mother and everybody alive. We were all confused and hopeless. We were all doomed! Scheduled for imminent destruction.

A whole life of promise, hope and ambitions went in exchange for sleepless nights, hopeless days eaten up by the silence of death, for a few minutes of pleasure. The same minutes I was about to take in exchange for the rest of my life. The same minutes my father took. And Koto, poor Koto. Kintu was on the floor in Boko's room trying to cry the situation away, but this type would not go away after a gallon of tears had been shed. I always admired him, now I didn't want to think of being him.

A lot of questions came into my head and I did not know whom to ask. Kintu was in the depths of bawling; Boko was too traumatized by grief, and Lydia was practically pouring out her gut as she yelled beyond her tongue's capacity. I wondered what Helen was doing. I wondered what Kintu's mother would say if and when she heard the news. I wondered what my mother would do if she heard I was HIV positive. I don't even think any of them could answer the questions, because nobody knows why they do what they do when they do it. Only God. I think.

There was silence in the room, a vacuum, and I could hear all the noises and the wailing, but they were not loud. It was as if the entire room was my head and the echoes rang as words, thoughts and question strike the walls. Maybe all this was just my mind. Doing what? I feel I am going crazy. I am losing it. I am in a bubble about to burst.

At that moment, a thought came to me; it practically walked into the room. I saw it with my own eyes, but didn't know what it looked like and it made me acknowledge what was right, what was important. It gave me one answer that answered all the questions. *Go to church*, it said. Church? I am really crazy now. Totally. Other answers came too.

I remembered my mother and my father. If they died, what would I do? I had been crazy to leave them when they needed me most. My mother always told Shola and I that we were the greatest gift God had given both her and my father. She said my father told everybody on the streets that he had a son, the day I was born and that he would sit by my cradle whenever he heard me mutter. She said he told her he always wanted to be there for me. He listened to my breathing flicker like the wings of a moth beating against the light through the night hours for the first month I was born. He wanted to be the best father he could ever be. The night he told Shola and I the infidelity story, he said the first thing that came to his mind was "what will happen to my children?". He said he would do anything to take the shame, the despair away. He would gladly die to see to it that my mother was not infected to enable her to be there for us. He hated himself for it. But I did not believe it nor did not want to believe he was sorry enough. There is no forgiveness in such an act of desolation.

My mother told me on the phone when I called her yesterday, that when my father got home and found out that I had left, he cried. He said all his children were gone. He said it was entirely his fault. He said he deserved it. I was somehow happy that he cried, but there was something in me that made me feel guilty. My father crying because of me. Shame, Shame on me. He found it immensely hard and uncomfortable to express his feelings, his face was chiseled soberness. My father believed in facts and did not hesitate to give his mind, but not his feelings. My mother was the spokesperson in those matters. She interpreted his mood and feelings to everyone else. The thought of him crying seemed surreal.

"When your father got home, he asked for you as he always does," my mother said in her usual spokesperson role.

"And what did you tell him?" I demanded.

"That you finally left for school in Uganda."

"Yeah."

"He cried", she said as if she was about to cry.

"Sorry about that", trying to hide my guilt wrapped up in shame.

"There is no need to be sorry, but do you know what that means?" she hummed into a pause.

"What does that mean?" I asked her in anticipation of an answer.

"It means he is a human being and he loves you," she declared as if she was whispering.

"Of course, I know he is a human, he is my father!" I tried to enforce since I felt she was trying to make me sound like a child again.

"I know you know. But do you know that humans make mistakes; they fail, they get weak and they need forgiveness?"

"Yes, mommy I know and what is this all about? Did he say I am angry with him? What has he done again this time?" I replied trying to control the tremble in my voice.

"He is my husband and I love him and it was I he offended not you or your sister, but you have a grudge against him. You have to learn how to forgive because people fail and everybody makes mistakes. You keep on acting as if nothing is wrong, but I can..." she was almost yelling.

"Mommy, can we please stop talking about this thing again, you keep on mentioning it! I have nothing against him!" I interrupted losing my temper.

"Ok. Topic closed!" She said with a disappointed voice. After the conversation, she cried about it, on the phone and I could not tell her to stop because it would sound cruel. I felt very guilty and somewhat empathetic, but I was still angry. Angry at myself for not wanting to forgive him. I felt a red-hot anchor of anger attached to my amber heart had been lodged in the bedrock of unforgiveness. I couldn't do much about it. It is fire out of control! I am addicted to it.

My mother always told me that I can choose to be who I want to be because every choice I make will lead me to another choice and in the long run there will always be a consequence for my choices. Life is made up of a series of choices then, not huts. And every choice I make has consequences, good or bad. She wanted me to forgive my father. I told her I didn't know how and she said I should just decide in my heart to do so. I should choose. Every time I want to hate, I should remember to choose to forgive him. It had not been successful. She said I would turn out worse than him if I decided to hate him because hate is a draining connection that sucks out good and installs evil.

I have always wished I were free, free from everything. Hate. Love. Life. Everything.

I have always wished I could know what goes on in people's minds and why they act the way they do. Sometimes I even try to ask them, but they give me the wrong answer. Maybe they don't know how to express it, or it could be that I do not know how to understand their answers, or I just simply don't want to understand them. What makes them smile when everything is lost? Why they bother living their lives when nothing is certain?

My mother never shows she is hurt and my dad never admits he is wrong, and Shola is always gossiping. Whenever I asked *why* they always denied it, or maybe I am the one who thinks they denied it. Maybe they are not who I thought they were; maybe everything was just an infestation in the mind. My mother said I deny the fact that I am angry with my father. I am not angry, but I hate him. I don't want to, though.

I remember asking Boko why he was always smiling as if he had some money waiting for him to inherit, but he always said, *this is the day that the Lord has made, I will rejoice and be glad in it*! Another uncertain day. He said it was a verse from the bible.

"You mean the verse makes you happy?"

"No, it reminds me to be happy."

"Really?"

"Yes. What else can I afford to be? It is cheaper to be

happy."

"Interesting."

"Honestly, it is only God that can give anyone peace and happiness, it's called 'Joy.'"

"And how much does that cost."

"Only costs believing in God; that he has your interest at heart and will always be on the lookout for you. After that you just have to lean back and relax. He is in control."

"Sounds like opium."

"But it's not. It's faith, trust and assurance of love; God's love. It never fails, it always builds up, never destroying."

When I woke up feeling empty this morning and I stared at the charcoal drawing on the wall, the entire drawing was a breath of fresh air and it blew in like a cool inspiration before an angry and violent storm. If I could meet God in person, I would have congratulated him for creating such a lovely day. The type that comes before everything gets flushed down the toilet. It's almost like Christmas day followed by the after blues. Perfect and rotten. It was as if there were two people in me with opposite feelings. The hopeful and the messed up.

It seemed as if it was the first day of my life and I could not wait to call my mother to tell her how much I loved her, and how sorry I was even though she never showed her hurt. I could not wait to give my father a hug, he would probably think I was crazy, but I didn't care. For the first time in a long time, I loved the colourlful sky. The warmth of the golden sun in white hidden behind the cloudy colourless sky; the conversations of the birds and the songs of people laughing in the streets. To my amusement, I also appreciated Boko's hymns blaring out from the bathroom. Was that Joy? It only lasted a few minutes.

It could be that everything was meant to be enjoyed because God made it and he made it beautifully; the air, the people, the day and everything. Everything seemed wonderfully beautiful, but I felt something was strangely missing. Something that would make the beauty complete. That began to dampen my mood. The pessimistic rot began to take over. I needed to find a way to strangle it.

I was slightly frightened; I thought I might be losing my mind. Since I kept contradicting myself, I got out of bed and started singing 'Amazing Grace', it sounded like an old nursery rhyme that I loved years ago; it was as if I found the words again. I think Boko was surprised because he stopped singing. I heard the shower turned off and the toilet door open. There was a knock on the door.

"Tola, is that you?" His curious voice asked.

"Mr. Boko, come in!" I called out in the radiance of jubilation.

"Are you ok?" he asked and I wasn't sure if I was.

"I am great", I replied teasing.

He was very puzzled about my behaviour this morning and wondered what was the matter. I explained, how everything seemed to be so beautiful and how grateful I was to be alive. I decided to follow Boko to church, though I just said it to make him smile. But now I really did want to go.

"God is about to do a new thing in your life," he said as he turned back to finish off with whatever he was doing in the bathroom, probably singing in front of the mirror.

Ironically, God had done something new in Kintu's life! I felt like I had been stupid to have ever admired anything since things appear to be good at first then it all comes crashing down before your eyes.

Kintu dropped us off at Kampala Pentecostal Church. He seemed more relaxed and less frightened about the morning's occurrence. We dropped Lydia off at the hostel earlier, the drive was silent and very long. Kintu consoled himself and Lydia that they would go for an HIV test on Monday morning, though we all knew the incubation period took a while, everybody just had to make do with it.

I asked him to come with us, and he gave me a shallow laugh and stared at Boko in envy. Boko smiled to enforce the invitation, but he just told us to pray for him. I wanted to follow Kintu since it seemed wrong for him to be alone, but I also wanted to attend the church service. I really didn't know why.

"Maybe I'll be there next week, I'll be back to pick ya'll at 12", he said with his rap tone. He had a frail presence about him as if he had something very important to attend to. Maybe a confrontation with his mother.

"Why don't you come with us, just for today? Since we are new, we will all be strangers here", Boko tried to justify in order to find a common ground.

"Nope, maybe next time!" Kintu interrupted in a hurry, stealing a quick glance at his watch.

"So where are you going now?" I was curious enough to ask.

"Home," and waved us goodbye as his car sped off the driveway. His Toyota Corolla brushed by the sun as it took a fast turn into the main road and burned away into the humming voice of the church choir in the early service.

Boko readjusted his tie as though he was about to meet an important person. I adjusted mine too just in case. He told me that we should pray for Kintu because he must be in a very bad state, though he does not want to show it. I agreed.

The church was of an average size, but the crowd was big, seemed as if we were queuing to enter a new club. The good thing was that the crowd was not an aggressive one. We all strolled into the church gracefully, like saints going to heaven, leaving behind our evil ways, at least for an hour or two.

I guessed a lot of the people who came to church might be actors and actresses; Kintu had once played a role here before. We entered the cinema-like church. I looked around at the smiling faces, and it made me wonder what heaven would be like. I tried to picture what some of those smiling faces might really look like when they are far away from the church or what they do when they are on their own, but I gave up. It was not constructive.

We sat in the middle of the church on the overhead above the main auditorium. After singing, clapping and giving our offerings, we finally sat down and a pastor with a heavy accent came on the platform. I don't remember his name, but he was introduced. I wasn't paying too much attention, so I don't remember what he was preaching about, but he seemed to be very upset. I think he was upset about people taking God and the work of Jesus Christ for granted. Two girls and a guy sat in front of me and they spoke to each other throughout the service, pushing, pointing, speaking loudly and chuckling, like retards.

I tried to listen to the echoing voice in the loudspeaker, but my eyes wandered away from the pastor and I stared at the painting on the wall. It was an artist's impression of scenery with birds, palm trees and a beach; it was beautiful. There was a crack in the upper right corner of the altar. I thought the offerings should pay for that to be fixed.

There was something about that moment I don't understand; all I knew was that I had been very ungrateful and that I was empty and alone. As if there was more to life than just this. I stared at Boko, but he seemed to be absorbed into the sermon. He was smiling and seemed peaceful, something I think only God could explain. It was a smile and peace I longed for, as much as I wished to see through Koto's eyes as a child. As the preacher went on about how Jesus came to die to take away all our sickness, diseases, our shames and failures; I remembered my mother. She always had the same peaceful smile on her face, as if all was well. With all the treatments and episodes; she would still give a graceful smile every time our eyes met. It always neutralized my apprehension. She smiled even in pain. The smile was a smile of confidence in God since both my mother and Boko were certain of God and what He could do. I feared He had already let me down. Or maybe I was the one who let God down.

"He can heal you, change you, deliver you, restore you. He will never leave nor forsake you and He can make you whole", the preacher listed as if he was reading an invisible note as he stumped in short steps up and down the altar.

"Jesus came and died so that you can be free", he called out in a peaceful rage as he pointed his hand at the crowd. I felt as if it was me, he pointed to, so I looked around to see if they were all looking at me. Me and my critical self.

No one was.

"This morning, I want you all to hear the voice of God in your spirits; I want you to search your heart this morning. There are some of you who are angry, some of you who are hurting, some who are empty. You feel hollow deep down inside, you feel worthless. There are some who are just ignorant, clueless and you just don't know and you just don't care..." and he went on as though he was invoking an incantation. I could not help but feel he was talking about me.

The choirs started singing and they sang like angels. One of the voices sounded like my mother's and it gave me goosebumps. The purple voice caressed my heavy heart.

I started sobbing.

"Hear the voice of Jesus calling, he can help you, he is the only one who can help you. No one will understand you, but he will. He made you. He can wipe away the tears and wash away the pain, he can fill you up, make you valuable because you are valuable to him; you are priceless to him, he loves you and that was why he did not hold back even his own life for you...God love you!" the Pastor declared in a bold and almost defiant manner.

It seemed I was alone in the hall for a moment and I cried out loudly. I did not care who was watching; the girl with the braids sitting to my left, the two girls and the guy chatting in front or Boko on my right. I cried because of my mother, because of Koto, because of my father and Kintu, and everybody. I cried because I was angry, I cried because I felt alone and I cried because I was clueless, there was so much I did not understand. I cried because I was crazy. I also cried because God irritated me and I cried because He has always cared for me and he had always been there, even when I thought I was alone.

He was the knock on the door. He was the voice in my room. He was the answer to my questions. He was the silent voice in my mind that told me everything would be alright. He was the calming voice that blew through the raging of my confused thoughts. He was also the same voice that told me to come back home; home to hope, home to faith. I felt warm waves roll through my body as tears burnt my face. Tears heated up over the years by the hurt and confusion, by the glowing wrath of my amber heart. He was the voice of my dreams telling me to be free. Free from the burdens.

10

The world is built on excuses. I was born. I was born black. I was adopted. I was born black and broken and now nothing really matters anymore. Absolutely nothing. My excuse is that the world is a dark miserable place to live where everyone is confused and nothing is concrete. Every person you see, even those with truthful eyes that are glazed over with love have secrets that will tear you to shreds. Their eyes smile because they love you and their mouth is held back from telling you the truth about who you truly are because of the silent hopes that you will never find out. For a selfish reason, for loves sake, whichever, but behind those happy eyes glazed over with affection, the truth is crying to come out at you and confront you, face to face.

***

His words tore out parts of his being as his heavy eyes tried to conceal his unbearable agony. His voice wove through the room like a spirit in search of a body. My ears refused them by virtue of my disbelief. Am I not my father's son? As the light departed from his voice, his eyes echoed what seemed a memory. The day he first held me in his arms, not as a newborn in a hospital ward, but as a toddler rescued from a schizophrenic mother on a garbage dump hollering into his heart that so longed for a son. Like a kind thought, he placed me forever in his embrace. Though I remained in his embrace, he knew it would never be the same again because my eyes must have spoken the disappointment and the fact that he would forever be to some extent a stranger to me. Though bound by the prickly chains of love and gratitude of always being there in some form or the other; a divide was forged in the conversation. One drawn in blood: we don't share the same blood. One that cannot be reversed, unspoken or undone. The divide, however, explained everything that had ever occurred. The strange stares at the family home in Abeokuta, the sly joking remarks about me being ‘imported' and the fact that I possess features that look neither like my father's nor my mother's: my height, my complexion, my feet, my eyes. My grand aunt's eyes that clawed at me at every family event, like a predator guarding its cubs against a wayward prey. That moment my heart weighed a ton and dragged behind me like an unwanted suitor. It felt like lava coursed in my veins. My head floated in the vapour of confusion. The taste of oxygen in my nostrils died out and everything went blank. Blank like nothing. Like an empty thought floating in the ether.

***

“If you have never accepted Jesus Christ as your Lord and personal Savior, come now. Come just as you are, he doesn’t care what you have done or what you have not done. Just come. Hear his voice calling, come here to the front, and don’t be ashamed. If you are ashamed of him in public, he will be ashamed of you before God on Judgment Day…” the voice announced in the loudspeaker.

I was still crying with my face in my palms when I felt Boko's affectionate hand on my back, it sent shivers. It was a familiar hand similar to a déjà vu.

"Tola, do you want to go to the front? I can go with you." He encouraged, as he tried to console me with his hand rubbing my shirt creating ruffles. I nodded ‘yes'; the girls with the braids who we prayed within groups of three earlier in the service made way in a slow motion of empathy. We stood up silently and walked our way down the stairs into the aisle. I was still crying and Boko kept telling me everything would be all right and I believed him, I don't know why I just did. The ushers along the way kept pointing to the altar with cheery gestures.

I didn't see anyone's face; all I saw was the altar in front of the church. The aisle looked like a bush path, and the people in the rows and columns of chairs were like grass stretching far beyond the horizon. I felt as if I was walking down the 'Grandfields of the ancestors,' out of the playhouse, as Koto elucidated, but not into the workhouse. I felt as though I was walking into a marvellous light—a light that had been shining at the end of the tunnel all these years. A light that would help me see through all the confusion and chaos in my life and mind. It glowed brightly with warmth, radiating in pulses like my heartbeat. I walked faster to get into the light sooner, and I wasn't in the Grandfields. I felt as if I was on a road surrounded by light, warmth, and order. I felt at home, like on the living room couch. The way I felt on Lenana Peak with Christie by my side, staring at the clouds with the sun shining on us. It was freedom. It was where I belonged.

In front of the church, another Pastor who gave me a fatherly hug met me and I cried even harder, but I cried because I was relieved. Relieved of what? I just couldn't explain. It made me wonder the last time my father hugged me. The Pastor spoke to Boko and they shook hands and then they hugged. Boko hugged me and I realized there were a lot of people who came forward. There were many faces and I thought I saw Lydia's face, but I was not sure. I just wanted to be there in front of the altar and nowhere else. I felt my heart getting lighter and lighter as the pulsating died down.

We all knelt and the Pastor prayed. As he prayed, I felt as if it was the first second of the first minute of the first day of my life. It was as if a heavy weight had been lifted off me, I felt new and alive. I felt light like a butterfly floating in the breeze of an early morning sunrise washed with the hopes that a new day brings. There was a great peace within me that I could not point my finger to. I just accepted it; that Jesus cares for me, that he loves me and that he has forgiven me and all my sins. Unforgiveness. Little birdie. All forgiven. I even felt it in my heart that I would never feel empty again. I felt so vibrant with life.

It is amazing how life can be what you make it, yet so far away from what you want it to be. It is also amazing how one day you are this and the next day you are that. Life is strange, weird, and it is so amazing how I ended up in front of the altar kneeling, believing in God; the same God I hated a few hours ago. The same God who made all this happen.

As we repeated the prayer of our confession after the Pastor, the choir reduced their voices and it sounded as if it was the wind singing a song with its blowing. I liked it and everything seemed just right, I did not hate my father anymore, and there was a sigh of relief in my mind as I repeated the words. What did I hate him for? What did he do wrong? I am not sure. I don't know!

"Upon the confession of your faith, you are now a new creature in Christ Jesus, the old has gone and the new has come. May the peace of God which surpasses human understanding go with you, be with you and live in you, in Jesus' name"

And the entire congregation responded with a loud and applauding, 'amen'.

On our way out, the crowd seemed more in haste to leave the building, since there was a little more tugging and pushing. I tried to walk close to Boko, but the crowd seemed to be pushing us apart. He had the same look he had; the same excitement he had on his face when we met in the airport in Nairobi. I guess he was happy for me. He dragged his way through the forceful crowd and around a group of people who had decided to have a conversation in the middle of the flood of people. I was curious to know what they were talking about that could not wait till they went outside; I tried to tune to their voices, out of the echoes and laughs. I thought I heard them say something about a red car in an accident.

Outside, the day seemed cloudy with the sun barely shining. The heavy shoulders of the grey clouds held it back. The matatu drivers were calling out the names of their destinations, in an attempt to get clients to board their rundown minibuses, but it seemed their clients were more interested in the breaking news.

"What?" A woman embellished the shock.

"Yes, a serious accident. I think it was actually a suicide," the man tried to deduct.

"It must be one of those drunkards who has been drinking the whole night. They always drive like mad people with loud music; things money will do to this country", I heard another voice in the crowd say.

"The accident is very serious, you can't tell whether the car was red or it was the driver's blood", A young man exaggerated his face clocked with sympathy.

"It is one of those rich men's children, maybe he was on drugs," someone else was explaining at our back as though he was fishing from his own personal experience.

We were unable to get the full story since people were speaking in a mix of English and their native languages. We asked a lady who seemed not to be interested in the entire ruckus taking place in front of the church. she said she was not sure, but she thought a young driver crashed directly into the wall of a shopping mall down the road. The car was crushed like a tin can she concluded, with such detail, as of one who had been at the scene earlier. She looked disgusted and pushed us aside to head to the more important things she had planned for the day.

There had been an accident because police cars were driving toward the end of the road, and a huge crowd of idle and curious people were practically running after the police to catch the event live as it unfolded.

I sat on the step next to Boko; trying not to entertain my fear, as the curious crowd pushed their way to their diverse directions. Boko was silent; he seemed to be trying to examine something in his mind, with his eyes staring at the sky as if the conclusion was there.

“I wonder what the outcome of Kintu’s test will be?” said Boko as he sat next to me on the step. He looked at his watch in a rush and I looked at mine, it was eleven minutes after twelve.

“Isn't there meant to be about a few months incubation period?" I replied as he took a deep breath.

"I don't know, you are the one who wants to study medicine or architecture!" He remarked almost sarcastically and incoherently.

***

Since I could learn to walk and talk, I have always wanted everything to be perfect. I have always wanted to be at peace with everybody. I wanted a world where everyone was entitled to smile and they would all shake hands like good old neighbors when they passed by each other on the streets. I always wanted my mother and father to be in love and sneak away from my sister and me every time to have their time alone, while both my sister and I were absorbed into the TV. I always wanted the sky to be blue so that I could go and play soccer with my friends on the field and I always wished that the ball would keep coming to me so that I would be able to score all the goals and be the hero of the game. I always wanted everything to make sense, to be logical, to have a reason and a purpose. Why should anything be without a valid reason? Why mental disorder without a logical reason. Why?

Sometimes I try to see myself in the future, as the greatest Doctor that ever lived and I imagine that after I die my great-grand-children and other students will have to take an exam based on my accomplishments before they can ever dream of becoming Doctors or 'a great thinker' for that matter. I believed I would smile down from heaven every time they were giving tribute to me. But can a crazy person become a great Doctor or is it an architect? Maybe I can combine both. I can build people. Yes, I will build people!

***

It came to me today, like advice from someone I knew. Life can never be perfect. A perfect life would be a boring life; everything would be predictable and there would be no need to think, to evaluate, to grow, to change or to dream. There would be no need for making choices or meeting new challenges. To appreciate. Life would be like a painting painted in white- there would be nothing to see- just a blank canvas to stare at and lie about what I thought I saw but did not see.

The imperfection makes me appreciate the goods things, just as the different shades of grey give life, texture and a feel to a painting. I guess life is just like the picture my mother gave me; it is black and white, with shades of grey and shades of white. Could that be why she gave it to me?

I will never fully understand the drawing even when I think I do.

"Boko, do you think I can be the one to find the cure for AIDS?" I asked to break the silence.

"I guess you can, if no one else does that before you graduate, but it will demand a lot of work and prayers, I think." He finally said after a long pause. I nodded hopefully.

"I better call my dad to thank him"

"Your dad? Thank him? For what?"

"For everything."

A skinny lady wearing an oversized blouse holding a bag of popcorn came to me, ignoring Boko.

"Hello. Can you please give me some money?" She demanded in a boring voice. I was caught off guard by her request and I stared at her for a while. She seemed shy because of the big patches of rashes on her skin and her head looked like a skull, which she kept scratching.

"What do you think? I just give out money? What do you want to use it for?" I asked her. She did not reply for a while but kept rubbing her eyes with the back of her hand when she was not scratching.

"To buy something to eat," she almost whispered. I did not feel like giving her anything, but something made me want to because I felt I wouldn't want God to deny my request even if I didn't look like I deserved it. I looked at Boko and he was just staring at the lady as though she was scaring him. I opened my wallet and handed her a 1000-shilling note.

"Wow, thank you," she smiled. "God will help you!" She stated and walked towards the direction of the accident.

"God help you too," I whispered in pity. I was still staring at her skinny body in the oversized blouse when Boko shook my leg violently.

"She's an angel!" He yelled as though he had been suffocating. He distracted me and when I looked back at the direction she went, she was nowhere to be seen.

"God! She just disappeared; did you see that!" He yelled and stood up pointing at the direction like he was running mad.

"No. How do you know?" I asked a little confused because the lady was strange, but did not look like an angel to me.

"No? Didn't you see the wings and her eyes?"

"No."

***

Sweet like the light of the sun sipping through the morning clouds onto the face of the darkest night, a hint of relief came like an itch that craved a good scratch, but the scratch had taken out a huge chunk of flesh. Where the itch once stood was a gaping raw wound flaring devilishly red like the mouth of a volcano. Never to be silenced again. She didn't have HIV, she had cervical cancer. They are not my parents, I am adopted. I am not Nigerian; I don't know where I am from. My mind seemed to have a mind of its own. I don't know what is real or true. God, I am really broken.

“You are not in Kampala; you are with us in Nairobi at home.”

“It’s not real?” I am perplexed and can feel the couch in the living room in Nairobi at the back of my head.

“I think he is having another episode...I called Doctor, but he’s not in the office...” my mother’s voice tremored with worry and I could feel her hovering around the couch.

“Son, are you ok?” His voice heavy with worry as well.

“I...I don’t know”

“Talk to me...” he firmly stated gripping my hand.

“I think something is broken...I think I’m crazy.”

"No, you are not. It's schizophrenia. The doctor said it might be hereditary, that’s why we had to tell you the truth...but you will be fine.”

“Boko said God...an angel...Koto...”

“What Tola? What?” His anxiety wrapped voice demanded as a warm teardrop tapped my forehead.

“I don’t know. I really don’t know...”

ABOUT THE AUTHOR

Olutayo K. Osunsan is an academician and author. He holds a Bachelor's degree in International Business Administration, a Master of Business Administration with a focus on Human Resources, and a Doctor of Philosophy in Management Science, specializing in Business Management.

Since 2004, Olutayo has had a notable career in academia, progressing from the position of teaching assistant to his current role as an Associate Professor. His tenure includes appointments at several esteemed Ugandan institutions, including Kampala International University, Victoria University, Africa Renewal University, and Cavendish University Uganda.

Olutayo has authored ten books between 2004 and 2021, encompassing a range of genres from poetry to academic texts. His literary works include "Strange Beauty" (2004), "The Poet in May" (2006), "The Life of One" (2010), "The Alchemy of Butterfly Memories" (2011), "The Life of Another One" (2013), "Business Communications" (2014), "This Happiness" (2015), "Leo" (2019), "Internationalizing Growth" (2020), and "The Integrity Clause" (2021). Some of his writings have been translated into various languages.

Beyond his academic pursuits, Olutayo's literary works often reflect his Christian faith, his deep appreciation for the African continent, and his insights into the human condition, exploring themes of personal struggle and growth.

In the realm of research, Olutayo specializes in quantitative social research. His areas of expertise include Management, Entrepreneurship, Small Business, Internationalization, Emotional Intelligence, and more recently, Innovation and Transformational Leadership. His scholarly work has been published in numerous peer-reviewed journals, both locally and internationally. Olutayo serves on the editorial committees of several journals and has been appointed as an external examiner at multiple universities.

From January 2019 to May 2022, he held the position of Vice Chairperson on the Executive Committee for the Children's Sports Charity Academy (CSCA). Currently, he is a board member of STEM, a Malawi-based community development organization.

Embracing the philosophy of lifelong learning, Olutayo adheres to the principle that mental renewal leads to personal transformation (Romans 12:2). In his personal life, Olutayo is married to Judith Nabirye Osunsan. They are the parents of three children: Hannah, Bethel, and Raphael Osunsan.

Made in the USA
Columbia, SC
11 November 2024